MYSTERIOUS TALES OF THE UNEXPLAINED

VOLUME II

Patricia Miller

Copyright © 2022 by Patricia Miller

ISBN: 9798433598829

All rights reserved. No part of this book may be reproduced in any form or by any means, including photocopying and recording, or by any information storage and retrieval system, electronic or mechanical, except for brief passages quoted in a review, without the written permission of the author.

The characters and events in this book are fictitious. Any similarity to real persons, living or dead, is coincidental and not intended by the author.

Also by Patricia Miller

Mystery Collection:

Mysterious Tales of the Unexplained: Volume I

YA Science Fiction Romance Trilogy:

Joshua: Life After Theos
Joshua: Breaking Free
Joshua: Between Two Worlds

Follow Patricia on:

Facebook.com/patriciamillerauthor
Instagram: @patriciamillerauthor
Website: pmwritescom.wordpress.com

ACKNOWLEDGMENTS

THIS BOOK IS DEDICATED to my great-nephew, Noah, and great-niece, Rylee, who have developed their own special love for books. I love you both. Keep reading.

Many thanks to the following people who have provided support and assistance with the publication of this book. Whether it be creative support, illustration assistance, beta reading, or ARC reading, I am incredibly grateful to:

Danielle Sawat, Liz Straus, Lisa Burrell, Heather Agar, Lacy Gallagher, Keri Stratton, Jennifer Kaczor, Amy Vavrock, Joni Turner, Kim Crosby, Robin Ginther, and the Northeast Ohio Educational Services Commission.

I wish to thank my coworkers for their support during the writing of "Scary Mary," and Amy Bertini, for being an idea soundboard during the writing of "Mystery Weekend at Morehead Mansion," and for her unwavering friendship.

I am incredibly grateful for the technological and creative assistance from Linda M. Au and Todd Engel. I am eternally thankful for their invaluable help.

Special thanks to Betty Ann Harris for her brilliant marketing of my publications.

Illustrators

Front Cover: Ryleigh Grewell

Back cover: Kaylee Dennis

"The Spiral Staircase": Rowan Wills, Alexis Mamula

"Scary Mary": Ashton Carlisle, Ashlyn Alberts

"A Puzzling Mystery": Maria Hernandez, Ryleigh Hornbeck, Rilee Pershing

"Mystery Weekend at Morehead Mansion": Katie Mylius, Thamia Martinez Caldwell, Rowan Wills

CONTENTS

The Spiral Staircase	1
Scary Mary	85
A Puzzling Mystery	117
Mystery Weekend at Morehead Mansion	169

THE SPIRAL STAIRCASE

THE SPIRAL STAIRCASE

WITH A DEEP BREATH AND SIGH, twelve-year-old Rylee struggled to put one foot in front of the other, climbing the spiral staircase in the south tower of her mother's Victorian home. But was it the same staircase she was so fond of climbing? *This doesn't seem quite right. This handrail feels funny. Not sure how, just strange. What's on the walls? Those pictures weren't there before.* She scrunched her eyes, trying to focus on them, but it was too late. It had already passed out of her view. Whatever it was, the blur of its outline floated quickly out of sight. And her legs didn't feel like her own. They couldn't be her legs. Her legs weren't this heavy and so hard to move. And yet, she kept struggling upward. Nothing would keep her from her favorite part of the house.

Rylee had always loved to climb the tower staircase since she moved to her new home with her mother two years ago. From day one, it had been her part of the house. The tower was more important to her than her bedroom, which said a lot. She looked over the curve of the stairs and rail as she rose further and further upwards. She knew when she reached the top, the view from the windows far and wide would excite her as it had so many other times. That view was hers and hers alone. But, in her dream, she somehow felt she shared it with another.

As she looked down toward her feet, she froze in confusion, catching sight of a pink ruffle skirt bottom. The ruffle, which was attached to the dress she was wearing, in no way resembled any of her dresses. *What am I doing in this ridiculous outfit? This doesn't seem right.* Rylee shivered, as the soft cotton frock was way too light for the cool temperature of the stairwell. *Who talked me into wearing this crazy dress? I'm freezing!*

More and more excitement built up inside as she continued to climb steadily, despite each leg feeling like it weighed several pounds. *Wow. I'm exhausted tonight. Just keep climbing. You can make it. It's going to be so beautiful at the top.*

Rylee's legs grew heavier as she could barely lift them high enough to make it onto the last few steps. Strands of golden hair fell in front of her eyes. Fatigue overcame her, and her left foot became caught in the skirt ruffle, causing her to lose her balance. The wall on her left broke her fall. As she rested for a moment, she jerked away from the scratchy texture of the wall behind her. Startled, she reached her right hand back to touch the unfamiliar, rough surface.

***

RYLEE SLOWLY OPENED HER EYES and squinted at the ever-so-small yet bright stream of light that always seemed to find its way through her bedroom curtains, no matter how tightly shut. Surprised to find herself in her bed, she looked around the room for reassurance that this was her bedroom. The repetitious dream felt more real every time. Her right hand reached back behind her from her typical side-sleeping position as it did in her dream, to touch the wall. *There was no scratchy wall. It was that dream again!*

With no reason to get up in a hurry, Rylee much preferred lazy summer hours to the early rising during the school year. Yawning, she guessed it must be earlier than she thought, and her cell phone confirmed this. *Eight thirty? Who in their right mind gets up this early? More importantly, why am I up?*

Knowing she would never be able to get back to sleep, she rose, made her usual bathroom visit, and after dressing, stumbled through the hall and into the kitchen. Deciding it was way too bright in there, she reached over the sink and pulled the blind down halfway, and began to get herself a bowl of cereal. Early mornings just weren't her best times.

"You're up pretty early," her mom observed, standing at the sink.

"Trust me," she said, annoyed at her mom stating the obvious, "I didn't plan to be."

Her mom snickered while rinsing the recently washed dishes. Wiping her hands with a brightly colored dishtowel, recently divorced Ginny leaned against a counter opposite her daughter and surveyed her face. Knowing it best not to push, she poured herself a half cup of coffee and sat down at a relatively modern, wooden table with very straight legs. Rylee followed, sitting opposite her mother. Silence didn't bother Ginny, and right now, it was necessary to give her daughter some time to warm up to the day. After a few quiet moments, she tested the waters.

"Do you have plans for today?" Ginny hoped to convince her daughter to help out in the Victorian gift shop she ran, housed in their mansion's front parlor room area. Ginny could certainly use the help. And it was better than her sitting for hours on the steps in the south tower, which had become Rylee's typical pastime. She worried about her daughter spending too much time alone, not to mention her obsession with the tower.

"No, not really," answered Rylee. "Why?"

"It's just that Saturday can be a hectic day in the shop and—"

"Yeah," Rylee interrupted, answering much more quickly than her mother expected. "I can help."

"Wonderful," her stunned mother said, smiling at her daughter, who couldn't seem to manage to return one. Ginny knew her daughter didn't often smile first thing in the morning.

A bowl, spoon, and cereal boxes sat in the middle of the table. And the table sat in the middle of a rather large kitchen filled with cherry wood cupboards with glass doors and a matching island. One of the selling points for Ginny, when she bought this sprawling home, was the beautiful kitchen.

"Finish getting yourself something to eat and get cleaned up," Ginny added. "I'll open the shop, and you can come when you're ready, OK?"

Rylee nodded, grabbed her favorite crunchy cereal, and began to pour herself a second bowl as her mother made her way to the other side of the house and the Victorian shop.

***

GINNY FLIPPED OVER the OPEN sign on the shop's front door, pausing to appreciate the view of the harbor just ahead as the bright sun blazed through the window. Starting over in the small area of Misty Bridge Bay was a good decision as far as Ginny was concerned. She hoped the change to a small community would be for the best for both of them. Friendly people, good weather most of the time, and her little shop were favorites with tourists who visited throughout the year. Rylee had seemed happy too. She had a friendly group of friends and made good grades in school. So far, the choice seemed to be working out for them.

Ginny opened the cash register and filled it with change from her lockbox, hidden in a secret closet behind the counter. She grabbed a box from a back room, carried it into a corner area of the shop, and began to carefully lay lace placemats onto a shelf beside other lacy items. Ginny was very particular with her displays. She heard her daughter's footsteps enter the shop. Ginny's location was around a corner and just out of sight from the register.

"Mom," Rylee called. "Where are you?"

"Over here," her mother answered without looking away from her task. Ginny had the shelf about halfway filled.

Rylee walked over, grabbed the rest of the placemats from the box, and started to arrange them like her mother, only on the other end of the shelf. Ginny smiled at her daughter as a thank you. The corner of Rylee's mouth turned up, but only a tiny bit. Rylee knew precisely the way her mother wanted the displays to look.

"Mom, I had that same dream again last night," said Rylee without looking away from the lace in her hands.

"Really?" Ginny paused, knowing it best not to look away either. "Well, it's your favorite part of the house, so I guess that could be why you dream about it so often." Ginny hoped this was why.

"I guess." Rylee was hesitant in her agreement. "The weird thing is that every time I dream about the spiral staircase, things are kind of different. The pictures, texture of the walls, and little tables and stools on the landings and steps are always different. And the worst part about it is I never make it to the top in my dream."

"Interesting dream to have, that's for sure," said Ginny, sighing. "I can see that it bothers you, but it is just a dream. I hope you don't let it get to you too much."

"I'm trying not to let it. I've made a decision," Rylee said, finally shooting a smile toward her mother. "This afternoon, I'm going to go up to the top of that tower and sit and enjoy it.

Enjoying the top in real life might make up for the frustration of never getting there in my dream." Rylee had a way of staying strong in difficult situations, which today was no different.

The lace placemats looked beautifully arranged. Rylee returned the box to the storeroom, but it took its place among the empty cardboard boxes in the far corner this time. As she turned back, she heard the ring of the old-fashioned bell attached to the front shop door and made her way out to help her mom.

"Hello," said her mother, smiling at a couple who had entered and began to look around. "Welcome to Misty Bridge Victorian Treasures. Let me know if you have any questions."

After tourists entered the shop hour after hour, this was one of the busiest days in several weeks. Rylee had bagged several purchases during the heavy Saturday, and she and her mother laughed at how most of the lace placemats they had put out earlier that morning were gone. Ginny really knew what her customers liked.

Soon, the rush lessened, and Rylee asked to leave for the day. Expecting this, her mother agreed, adding that she wanted her to fill the gap on the shelf with more lace placemats before going. Without hesitation, she did as her mother asked, looking just as they did before, and quickly exited the employee-only door into a hallway leading back to their private living area. The area behind the shop was their haven, with several rooms and a large patio off the kitchen.

She grabbed a book with a brown-colored cover from her bookshelves, a favorite soft blanket, and rushed up the spiral stairs of the south tower, panting until reaching the top. She lifted one of the small windows, enjoying a slight breeze that moved her blonde hair off her shoulders. After taking in a massive breath of air from the bay, she sat and sighed. Rylee glanced her eyes over the fantastic bay view and then dropped them to begin to read about one of her favorite female sleuths, Kelsie Raymond.

***

GINNY SPOKE INTO HER CELL PHONE with a slight whisper. "Sarah, I have never heard of this legend before."

Sarah, honest and loyal, answered her bluntly. "Well, I'm not surprised by that. If the realtor shared it, they might not have made a sale."

Ginny furrowed her brows with anger. "That's dirty." She let her fingers run through her blonde hair, fluffing it up a bit.

"Maybe so. But I can't say as I blame them," added Sarah, knowing she had a solid point.

"Sarah, you have been my best friend since I moved here. Why on earth didn't you ever tell me?" Her tone was indignant, but it didn't bother Sarah, also clever.

"Ginny, listen to me. I have never believed in such things. And you just told me about Rylee's reoccurring dream. I never had any reason to tell you before. Until now, I thought of it as just a bunch of baloney." Surely Ginny wouldn't let something as lame as a legend ruin their friendship.

"I guess." Ginny looked around the great room she had added to the back of the house. She then walked out of it and into the older part of the Victorian home. "I love this place. I loved it from the first moment I saw it. I don't think hearing of a legend would have swayed me away from buying it."

"Honestly, Ginny. I wasn't keeping it from you," Sarah insisted. She was glad Ginny was calming down. "Anyways, the legend goes that a little girl lived in your home long before you and Rylee. I have no idea when this would have been, but my grandfather told me that the girl had some disease that made walking hard. Her brothers and sisters would always go running in the hills and through the woods, but she never could keep up. They said that she was sad because she would try and try to climb the hills and sometimes had to give up and sit down in exhaustion."

"Not much to that story, is there?" Ginny sarcastically said.

"Hold on. Hold on," Sarah said. "The legend goes on to say that she was closest to her oldest brother, not sure why, but that he died in some accident, and from that day forward, the little girl was devastated and never tried to play with the rest of her siblings or friends ever again. Grandpa might have been trying to scare me, but he said that she died young and haunted the hillsides, but that ending sounds like just something added to spice up the story. Rylee's dream of never getting to the top of the stairs and her legs being so heavy is what reminded me of it."

"Yes, there is that similarity," Ginny agreed. "But, that's a little bit of a stretch to Rylee's dream about climbing her favorite place in the house." Climbing hillsides and climbing stairs were different, but it was similar enough to nag at Ginny deep inside. She wasn't sure if she was glad or not to know. Now, to decide if she should tell her daughter.

***

RYLEE LAY ON HER BACK, sprawled on her bed with her head hanging over the edge. Upside down, she held her cell to her ear, laughing. Looking out through an extra-wide window, she enjoyed watching sunshine dance between the wind-blown tree limbs.

"That's crazy," she chimed in as her friend shared some story she heard through the grapevine. "Really? No!" Rylee sat up and smiled. "OK. I'll ride my bike over to your house. See you." And with a click, she ran from her room.

Halfway out of the house, she yelled back toward the kitchen to her mom. "I'm heading to Heidi's house, Mom. Be back in a couple of hours."

Ginny came out to the foyer just in time to hear the front door slam shut. She looked at the grandfather clock in the corner, glad to see that two hours would be just suitable for dinner time. With chili cooking itself in a Crock-Pot, Ginny decided to take this opportunity to do some research at the small Misty Bridge Bay library just across town.

The sign, an anchor painted blue with white trim, swung back and forth in the wind above her head. Ginny managed to pull the heavy door open and step in. The inside was a series of smaller rooms with worn carpet throughout.

The sunny day played games with her eyes for a bit as they struggled to adjust to the less brightly lit rooms and extended shelves. Having already asked for books on local history, she found herself in the very back of the building, in a corner where the floor made crackling noises beneath her steps. There was a slightly musty and old smell in this corner, and she noticed that some older-looking chairs were sitting angled toward each other, barely fitting between the shelves.

After pulling four books from a shelf, Ginny sat down in one of the old chairs in the corner and began to look through them, searching for anything written about her property. Lost in the pages, she barely noticed the sound of creaking floorboards heading in her direction. Startled, she looked up to see the head librarian standing a few feet from her, shelving books.

"I'm sorry I startled you," she said, smiling at Ginny. The lady was holding several books, reshelving them in their proper place.

Embarrassed, Ginny smiled back. "Oh, that was silly of me. I guess I got lost in this book."

"Can I ask what you're looking for?" asked the librarian. She had rectangular-shaped glasses frames and brown tight curls in her hair. "Wait a minute. I know you now. I didn't recognize you when you first came in, but you own that huge Victorian house over by the bay." Ginny nodded. "Oh, that place is beautiful. I bet you get a lot of tourists in your shop too."

"A fair bit, yes," answered Ginny. She looked back at the books in her lap. "Well, I'm looking to see if there is anything in these books about the history of my property. A friend told me there were some legends about it, but I hoped I could find out more."

"I don't think there's anything in any of these books about private residences in the area," she answered, smoothing down one of her curls. Ginny sighed as the librarian continued. "But, I do know who you should talk to." She smiled at Ginny with a gleam in her eye. "Bessie Brinkman, really nice old lady. She lives on the other side of the village. She's a book collector and knows more about the history of Misty Bridge Bay than anyone I know."

"Really? Do you think she would mind if I call her?" Ginny slid the books back onto the shelf.

"Are you kidding?" the librarian laughed. "She'd be thrilled. I really don't think she gets many visitors, I'd expect." The librarian started walking back through the labyrinth of aisles toward the main desk. "Here, follow me. I'll write her address and phone number down for you."

Back in her kitchen for dinner, Ginny sat with Rylee, who slurped chili from a bowl.

"Careful," she said. "It's hot."

Rylee blew on her spoon a little, but as usual for her, she couldn't wait long enough for it to cool. "It's so good."

"I know you like it, honey, but it's not worth burning your tongue over," said her mother as she grabbed an ice cube from the freezer and slipped it gently into her daughter's chili bowl.

"Thanks, Mom," Rylee said with a smile.

Ginny sat down. For a while, it was quiet while the legend swirled inside her head. Hesitantly, she decided to share her friend's information. "I was talking to Sarah the other day, and she told me something about our property." Rylee couldn't believe what she was hearing with every detail that came out, her eyes bulging larger with every word.

"Mom," said Ginny in between bites. "That's so interesting. Do you think this legend could have anything to do with my dream?"

Ginny took a deep breath. "I don't know if I would get my hopes up about it relating to your dream directly. But, it is within the history of this property and our house specifically. So, I think I'm going to check into it further."

"I want to do that too," said Rylee to her mom, who smiled and nodded back at her. "So, how do we do that?"

"We go over to an old lady's house named Bessie Brinkman

and talk to her about it," Ginny explained. "I guess she is the authority on the history of Misty Bridge Bay."

"Cool," added Rylee.

***

Rylee and her mom drove over to Bessie Brinkman's address, all the while a constant stream of conversation filled the car. Ginny hadn't heard her daughter talk this much to her in months. She couldn't get a word in edgewise, but Ginny liked it all the same. As they pulled up, the chatting ceased, and they both peered at a large, stone house with oddly shaped windows and slanted roofs. Rylee read the sign on the stone arch over the front walkway.

"Misty Bridge Manor," her daughter read aloud, then looked up. "Do you see how far back this house goes?" They both leaned to one side to see the depth of the home. "I think it's bigger than our house, Mom."

"It's a lot bigger than our house, Ry," her mom agreed. "And such beautiful, gray stone." Ginny paused to take in the magnificence of the structure. Her attention fell on the unevenly shaped windows, thinking they had to have special ordered them.

"This is out of this world, Mom," said Rylee with her lower jaw permanently dropped.

"It sure is," agreed her mom. "Well, we had better go in. Bessie is expecting us."

Rylee turned to her mom as they walked through the archway and up the front walk. "Thanks for letting me come with you."

"I'm glad you wanted to come. It's more fun with you along." Her mother smiled and put her hand on her daughter's shoulder.

The librarian was correct. Bessie was older, about seventy-five, Ginny guessed, and seemed excited to have company. She brought them drinks and pastries on a tray as they all sat down in what looked like the most enormous and richly decorated parlor room Rylee had ever seen.

The entire room was covered with the darkest and richest-looking wallpaper either had ever seen. Colors of dark burgundy and gold intertwined and perfectly matched the upholstery and curtains pulled back by cable ties beneath the threshold. Pictures in thick gold frames adorned the walls and appeared to be landscapes, some with horse carriages in them. Whether it be an end table or the coffee table, sideboard, or buffet, every table stood upon clawed feet.

"What a cool room," Rylee said, looking around, trying to take in everything.

Bessie chuckled a bit. "Well, thank you, young lady." After inviting them to sit down, Bessie continued. "Most of the furniture in here was left to me by my ancestors after they died. That buffet was my great-grandmother's, the end tables belonged to my aunt, and the little settee was a gift from a very close friend who has passed on."

Rylee turned toward her plate, reminded of the goodies in front of her. She smiled as she chewed on a chocolate petit-four, pleasantly surprised to learn of the creme filling inside.

"Now," said Bessie, turning to Ginny. "You own the beautiful Victorian home over on Bridge Bay Street, and you want to know about the history of your property. Is that right?"

"Yes," answered Ginny. "The local librarian said she thought you would be the best to ask."

"Hmm." Their hostess made this noise as she sipped her tea. She replaced her flowered cup on the equally delicate saucer, smoothed one of the many curls pushed up in her beehive of a hairdo, and cleared her throat. "What the librarian might not have told you is that I once was a history teacher back in my day, you see." She smiled with the pride that came with remembering her younger days.

"No, she didn't tell me that," answered Ginny. Rylee was half listening and half enjoying the pastries.

"Yes, and my ancestors have lived in Misty Bridge Bay for decades and decades." She paused for dramatic effect. "My grandmother had written journals about what her grandmother had told her about the village, and when she died, she left them to me." Bessie smiled with pride.

"Oh my," Ginny said. "You mean you know this village going back—"

"Farther than you can ever imagine," Bessie finished Ginny's sentence for her.

"That's amazing," declared Ginny. "How do you think you can help us?"

"The journals are exceptionally complete," said Bessie, again pausing for dramatic effect. "They talk about what was going on with nearly every family and property in the town, you see."

"My goodness," exclaimed Ginny. "How on earth did they have time to write everything down?"

Bessie snickered. "I'm told my ancestors were very good at knowing everything that went on and made it their job to keep track of it all in the journals. I think today we would call it nosey or being a busybody." This made all three of them snicker.

Their hostess got up and walked over to what looked to be an antique cupboard with curved legs, drawers, and compartments one would not think were compartments. She reached inside one and pulled out a long, thin key to unlock a large filing cabinet that looked more like a wooden safe. Inside, dark leatherbound books lined the shelves, far too many to count. Bessie slid a finger over them, left to right, and then chose a few.

Rylee couldn't help but comment. "Wow. Look at all those

books." She rose, set her plate on the coffee table, and walked slightly closer before Bessie closed and locked the cupboard.

"Oh my dear, that's only a few. I have a whole slew of books stored in cupboards all over this house," said Bessie. "Now, let's all sit down, shall we, and see what we can find out about you and your mother's beautiful property."

Rylee sat back down, but not before imagining tons of journals stored in tons of antique cupboards all through Bessie's extraordinary manor.

***

BESSIE PAGED THROUGH a few journal books before deciding on one in particular. Rylee and her mother leaned in close, eyes and ears peeled, not wanting to miss a single word that escaped the historian's mouth. Bessie read entry after entry aloud, when finally she closed the book, and the three sat in silence for a few seconds. Ginny broke the silence.

"Wow," she said with a deep breath. "Now, that's a lot to consider."

"I don't understand," Rylee said with a furrowed brow. What did your grandmother mean when she wrote 'evil walks the hills'?"

Bessie sipped her tea before she explained. "I think she meant that before the house—your house—was built on the land, many awful things had happened there. Earlier in the journals, she talks of a barn burning down, then of drowning, then the terrible accident of that little girl's older brother." Bessie paused to take a sip. "It could have just been an expression regarding all those terrible things that happened."

"But, wasn't the third incident later, after someone built our house?" asked Ginny.

"I'm not sure when that happened," said Bessie. "I would have to research that a bit more."

"My friend Sarah said that there was a little girl who couldn't run and play," said Ginny. "She must have suffered from some kind of illness."

"So far," said Bessie, holding up one of the journal books. "It doesn't say what ailed her."

"Bessie," said Ginny delicately, "Rylee has a reoccurring

dream." Ginny turned to her daughter. "Why don't you tell Bessie about it?"

Rylee was reluctant at first, but she decided she liked Bessie. She smiled and seemed like she would believe and accept the craziness of Rylee's dream. So she spilled all about it.

"I don't understand how Rylee's tower dream fits in with my property's history," said Ginny. "Indeed, if she couldn't run or play, she surely couldn't climb the tower either?"

"Well," added Rylee, "in my dream, I struggle to lift my legs to climb the tower. Maybe the little girl used to like climbing the tower too, but then was struck with some kind of illness."

"Yes," Bessie agreed. "That theory makes sense. Let me look into that a little more, and I'll get back to you."

Rylee pulled her stocking feet onto the couch and curled her legs, resting her chin on her knees. "I want to hear it all, Bessie." Each of the three smiled widely at each other.

Bessie reached over and patted Rylee's calf, smiling. "And so you shall, my dear. And so you shall." She looked at Ginny. "You might have a budding historian on your hands, Ginny."

"I just might," answered Ginny.

"I'll have to think about that," said Rylee, grinning. "That sounds like it might be cool."

Pizza ordered and devoured. Bessie read from the earliest journal retrieved from the cupboard so far, relating to Ginny's property with sodas all around, chips, and snacks covering the coffee table. It appeared weird to Rylee to have all of this sitting out on a coffee table in such an elegant room. But Bessie didn't seem to mind at all.

"This journal talks of men digging on the land. It doesn't say what they were digging, just that there was a lot of digging going on." Bessie read quickly and recapped what she read for the other two.

Ginny had her nose inside another journal. She nearly sprung from her chair. "There's more in this one about the digging early on, except towards the back; it doesn't mention digging. Then it goes into something about buying sheep and goats." She sighed.

"Sheep and goats?" asked Rylee.

Bessie nodded. "First of all, my ancestors had a habit of jumping all over the place in their journals, so I know it can get a little confusing. Now I will address the animals. Back in the old days, many people made money from raising animals. Plus, animals did a lot for people. They pulled the plows, provided fur with which to make things, and when they raised livestock, they provided food."

"Oh, wait!" said Ginny. "Hold on. Hold on. It picks up again." Ginny's eyes widened with delight.

"I'm not a bit surprised," said Bessie. "Read it aloud, Ginny."

For three or four hours, the three took turns reading from several journals. They were tired, rubbing their eyes and yawning. They became so engrossed with the journals that none of them noticed the rain patting upon the windows and pavement outside. They each closed their books, got up to stretch, and shared more of their findings thus far.

"Tunnels," said Bessie. "Who would have thought there could be tunnels hiding beneath properties? That's an exciting thought, isn't it?"

"I don't know if I would call it exciting or worrisome from my perspective," said Ginny.

"How could there be tunnels down under there?" asked

Rylee. "Wouldn't somebody find them when they dug out basements for houses?"

"That's what I was thinking," said Ginny. "How did they not find them?"

"I don't know," answered Bessie. "But, if they are down there, they might be hiding secrets." Bessie looked over her reading glasses as she did when she wanted to make a point.

"Secrets?" asked the wide-eyed, enthusiastic girl. "What kind of secrets could there be?"

"I don't know," said Bessie, looking from one to the other. "Do you want to find out?"

Rylee looked to her mom, and without saying a word, they each knew things would get really interesting now.

If the investigation of unknown secret tunnels wasn't intriguing enough, they each were startled by the noise of someone entering Bessie's place from the rear. A young blonde and kind of good-looking teenager, Rylee thought, blustered into the sitting room, obviously surprised by the presence of visitors.

"Aunt Bessie, can I have one of your fancy cupcakes from the counter?" he said, stopping mid-sentence. "Oh. Hello." His smile was obviously meant for Rylee, and she also noticed him.

As any mother would, Ginny sized up the young gentleman. She leaned over and whispered to her daughter. "He looks a little old for you."

Bessie answered the whisper. "He's only thirteen," she said, boasting an incredibly ornery smile. Bessie sat back and hid a smirk behind a journal as Ginny shot her a chastising look. Bessie's eyes danced above the journal, thoroughly enjoying the looks Rylee and her great-nephew Samuel were exchanging. This did not entertain Ginny.

***

GINNY MOVED ABOUT THE SHOP, darting here and there, in a hurry to make a savings deposit before the bank closed. Having forgotten to lock the door, behind her came the dinging of the bell above. She spoke as she turned to face the newly arrived occupant.

"I'm sorry. I closed five minutes ago," Ginny said, interrupted by what she saw before her, where stood a tall, thin, and, in her opinion, not bad-looking man in the vicinity of her age.

"Oh," he said back. "I didn't notice your sign." He turned to leave. "I'll come back tomorrow then."

"No," she stopped him. "It's OK. I am in a hurry to get somewhere, but if it doesn't take long, I can get you what you need."

He smiled. "Thank you." He raised his hand to his forehead. "My head's been pounding."

Ginny smiled as she quickly walked over to a shelf, grabbed a bottle, and gently tossed it to him. He caught it, looked down, and nodded.

"Thank you. How much?" he asked, reaching for his wallet.

"Tell you what," she said. "On the house since I'm in a hurry."

"Thanks," he said, wishing he had more time to talk to this pretty lady. "Well, I'll get out of your way," he said, smiling while backing out the door, waiting till the last second to look away.

Ginny quickly grabbed the bank deposit bag and rushed down the sidewalk after locking the shop door for sure this time. She didn't notice, but her new friend stood on the other side of the road, watching her as she went.

That night, Ginny and Rylee had a quick supper with an equally quick cleanup. As usual, Rylee disappeared into her room; Ginny was happy her daughter ate with her and didn't argue about after-dinner chores this night. They had only used a few dishes and with them rinsed, she was OK with letting them sit in the sink for now. Ginny sat on her front porch swing, gently gliding forward and back, while multiple details from the journals swirled around in her head.

She startled and jumped slightly, her racing thoughts interrupted by her cell phone ringing.

"Hello." Gina sat up straight on the swing. "Oh, Sarah." Ginny then listened. Surprised, she answered back, "Your older brother? That's who came into my shop for aspirin?" More listening followed, and then finally she stood. "He's visiting you?"

Sarah added a thought that Ginny found to be very exciting. "He can help you guys research your property." *Wouldn't that be nice? I wouldn't mind hanging out with him anyway.*

"What did you say his name was?"

***

Sarah's older brother, Ben, sat quietly in Misty Bridge Manor, listening as Bessie disclosed more information she had found in her journals. Ginny didn't want to miss one word with eyes and ears peeled again. Rylee and Samuel sat beside each other in seats off to the side in Bessie's parlor. The younger two listened off and on while playing with their cell phones and exchanging furtive glances. The rain had passed, and the evening was a bit damp.

"Ginny, I think you might find this very interesting," said Bessie, looking over top her reading glasses. "While I was researching, I discovered more about that little girl who couldn't walk well. I checked in several different references just to be sure."

"To be sure of what?" asked an impatient Ginny.

"Well, it seems that her older brother, whom she loved so very much, loved her back the same."

"But, you said he died in an accident of some kind?" asked Ginny. "How do you know for sure that he loved her very much?"

"By reading about how he used to carry her. In several of these entries, they refer to someone carrying her if she wasn't strong enough to walk," said Bessie. By her holding onto their gaze, they knew she had more to share. "I checked in several different journals and books, and I finally found some written about her beloved older brother."

"That's sad to think how she relied on him to carry her, and then he died," added Ben. Ginny moved with a start, not expecting him to join in. She was, however, pleased that he did.

Ginny looked from Ben to Bessie, furrowing her brow. "Yes, that's sad, but I don't see how that gets us much further," exclaimed Ginny.

"Ah, but you haven't heard the best part." Bessie paused, turned to the younger couple, and continued. "Rylee, I think you will want to hear this too."

Rylee took her gaze off her new friend and gave Bessie her full attention. It was quiet, and everyone was perched and ready to learn a critical piece of information. Tonight, Bessie had the fireplace lit, and the crackles of the embers added to the drama of the moment.

"I read, and I read," Bessie said sternly. "And eventually, I found something very, very interesting. It seems that the little girl often asked him to carry her to her favorite place of all."

Rylee covered her mouth with her hand as she gasped. Bessie turned to her and smiled, realizing the girl had figured it out.

"He used to carry her up the spiral staircase and up into the tower?" Rylee asked the question, all the while failing to believe it could be true ultimately.

"We still don't know a whole lot about it, but that's right," Bessie confirmed. "He used to carry her to a tower in her home. I hope to learn more eventually if I keep reading."

"It has to be. It totally explains my dream. It all makes sense," asserted Rylee.

Rylee and her mother looked at each other in awe. So, now there was a connection between Rylee's repetitive dream and this little girl in Bessie's journals. Rylee was completely quiet on the drive back to their home and for a good reason.

***

AT THE VICTORIAN SHOP, Ginny enjoyed a slow day for a change. The slow traffic gave her time to go over the books, do a little inventory counting, and ponder the fantastic discovery about the little girl who they thought once lived on their property. Ben became a staple of sorts, spending as much time with Ginny as possible. In the afternoon, he popped into the store to have a chat.

"Well, hello," he said as he meandered in, wearing jeans and a light blue button-up shirt. Hands in his pockets, as usual, his smile spoke volumes.

"Hi there," answered Ginny with an equally broad smile, thoroughly enjoying his blue eyes and thick, sandy blond hair.

"How has your day been so far?"

"It's been slow today, but that's been all right by me," Ginny answered. "I've managed to take care of some chores I had been putting off."

"That's good. Hey, I wanted to tell you that I talked to someone down at the county recorder's office who said they could help you locate the history of this property."

Ginny allowed her hands to run up and down the legs of her

jeans. She hardly noticed the warmth caused by friction and then paused as she struggled to get up to speed with what he meant. When she didn't respond right away, he explained.

"The county recorder's office keeps records of property histories. That means they might know what was built on your property before your house was there. They might even have records of tunnels if there really were tunnels."

"Really?" she asked. "Thank you for making that call." Her eyes danced at the idea of finding some concrete knowledge to help them understand what might be going on.

"There's no guarantee. I don't want you to be disappointed if there isn't as much information as you might want," he was sure to explain.

Ginny nodded. "I understand. "What do we do? Do we go over there or what?"

"Tell you what," he said with a flirtatious look. "After you close up shop, how about I take you out to eat, and we talk about a plan. OK?" Ginny wasn't going to turn down that offer. She liked him too much to do that.

***

The local diner was booming with patrons. Sunday afternoons usually meant all employed waitresses were working as many shops and businesses were closed. There wasn't much else to do in Misty Bridge Bay on a Sunday except eat out and walk along the bay. Ginny usually spent Sunday evenings alone and quiet, with her daughter often chatting via text messages with friends in her room. But, she decided this was a much better Sunday afternoon than usual.

Ben and Ginny sat in a quiet corner in the diner, finishing up soup and sandwiches. Once they devoured last sips and bites and plates were removed, they discussed plans. Furtive glances swapped back and forth as they talked.

"So, you say we should go to the county recorder?" asked Ginny. "They keep records, right?"

"Yes," answered Ben. "We probably can, at the very least, find out who bought and sold your land. I bet their records go back a long way."

"Bessie also says that we should check with the Bureau of

Land Management. There isn't an office in Misty Bridge Bay but twenty minutes away in Cloutan."

"She's quite a smart lady, isn't she?"

"Yes, indeed." Ginny took a sip of coffee. "I have to keep the shop open. I'm just not sure when I can find the time."

"Well," said Ben timidly. "I already thought of that, and I think I have a solution." He had hoped that his flirtatious smile would help sell his idea to Ginny. The look she gave him indicated a fair amount of suspicion.

***

THE FOLLOWING DAY, Ben walked from his sister's house, down the street, and to the business district. As trees disappeared, boats and seagulls appeared amid bright sunlight. It was another summer's day. He rounded a corner and peered down the road toward Ginny's shop. He smirked, delighted about the fact that he had talked her into his little plan. He pulled on the shop door and stepped in.

Ginny was buzzing around the shop, appearing a bit frantic.

Her daughter, Rylee, and her new friend, Samuel, stood between displays, watching her move back and forth giving orders.

"Mom," said Rylee, "we can handle the shop today. After all, I have watched it all by myself before. This time, I have help."

"I'm sure, but..."

"Ginny," Ben offered gently. "We should get going. I'm sure Rylee and Samuel will do just fine."

Ginny stood quiet, smiling at her young daughter. After nodding, she grabbed her purse and left, walking out in front of Ben. He looked back at the youngsters and smiled.

Rylee looked at Samuel. "Now, you get behind the cash register, and I'll tidy up the shelves." He stepped behind the counter as told. "This is the first time Mom has let me have someone else help me watch the shop. I don't want anything messed up."

Samuel raised a flat hand to his forehead and smiled. "Aye aye, captain."

***

The county recorder provided precisely the information Ben was expecting. They now had a list of names of all who bought and sold Ginny's property over the last one hundred years. But they were slightly overwhelmed.

"This is all very interesting, but I wish I knew what to do with it," exclaimed Ginny. She turned to face him directly. "I guess it's time to go to the Bureau of Land Management in Clouton. But, I probably should get back to the shop."

"Rylee and Samuel will be just fine at the shop," Ben insisted. "Come on, let's get on to Clouton. Let's get as much information today as we can."

She smiled at his dedication to her cause. It was hard for her to stay away from her shop for an entire day, but this gentleman, whose presence she very much enjoyed, persuaded her.

Later that same day, Ben walked her to her house long after her shop had been closed by the youngsters. The sun was starting to lay lower in the sky and afternoon shadows made the Misty Bridge Bay business district look rich and dark in color. They stopped in front of her large, Victorian house by the gate, which announced the stone walkway to the grand front door.

Ginny's property was a little bit of a walk to the harbor, but at night, when there was no one about, the gently lapping of water against boats and docks could be heard.

"I knew there was a chance at finding some interesting information, but I never counted on that much," he stated.

"I know," she answered. "Crazy to think that we were able to get copies of all the building and construction that happened on my property, not to mention the surrounding properties. There's so much to think about."

"What's next?" he asked.

She smiled in somewhat of a shy manner. She shrugged her shoulders as he moved closer.

"I know," he answered. "How about this?"

He kissed her gently. Ginny, although closing her eyes initially, opened them at the end. And she couldn't help but notice a curtain from a second-floor bedroom wiggling. She sighed, unsure if she should embarrass him with what she saw.

"Oh," he said coyly. "You probably thought I meant with the property information."

"That was what I thought we were talking about," she answered. They both chuckled. "I think we should take it to Bessie and go over it all with her."

"Good idea," he said.

"I think we ought to call it a night, Ben," said Ginny, looking up toward the window in question. "I think we're being watched. No, don't look," she said, grabbing his shirt before he could turn around. She smiled at him once more and let go of his shirt. "I'll let you know when that will be. I'm sure you'll want to be in on it."

"Of course," he answered as she moved away and strolled up the front walk to the door. "Talk to you soon." Before he turned to leave, he also looked up toward the second-story windows. He smiled and turned and walked back to his sister's house.

***

BESSIE WAS IN HER GLORY as she played hostess to Ginny, Ben, Rylee, and Samuel, who seemed most often by the side of his new twelve-year-old friend. They all sat around Bessie's large, antique dining room table, looking over the paperwork Ginny and Ben had obtained. Rylee looked around the dining room with the same excitement as when she saw the parlor for the first time.

"Bessie," she said. "I just love your house. It's so big and beautiful."

"Thank you, honey," said Bessie.

"Do you think I could have a tour of it sometime?" Rylee asked with a gleam in her eye.

"I think that can be arranged," answered Bessie. "Now, how about we get back to all these papers your mom and Ben came up with." Rylee nodded and turned her attention to the table.

"So, what does all this mean, Bessie?" Ben asked.

"There are so many bits of information to consider and so many ways to begin exploring," said Bessie. She pulled one paper in particular in front of her. "But, of all the maps you obtained, I think this one has the most clues. This map shows construction that occurred over a hundred years ago. And this one shows people with the same last name as the little girl whose parents purchased your property. I'm not sure what all these marks mean, but—"

Ginny cut her off. "Wait a minute. What do you mean by the same last name? We don't know the name of the little girl in the journals, do we?"

Bessie smiled, walked over to one of her glass-front cupboards, picked up a tattered old-looking journal, and sat down. She read from a page near the end. When she finished, all mouths were gaped open.

"Tuttle? Her last name was Tuttle?" Rylee asked.

"Yes," Bessie answered. "The same name that's in the information you found at the county recorder's office."

"So, cool," exclaimed Samuel.

"Yes," continued Bessie. "It's excellent when you have corroborating evidence from more than one source of information. That way, you know for sure you're on the right track."

Ben grabbed a different map from the center of the table and angled it for the others to see clearly. "Wait a minute. Look at this map. It shows your property, Ginny, but the property lines are different."

Ginny leaned in to look. "I don't understand."

Bessie explained to him. "They purchased your property but also your neighbor's property too. See," she pointed, showing the more considerable amount of land within the lines.

"And what are these marks?" asked Ginny. "These marks are different from the ones you say are property lines."

"Oh, that's easy. I know what they are," said Samuel.

Everyone looked up in surprise. Samuel was caught off guard and suddenly looked overly nervous having to explain, but after stammering a bit, he managed.

"Those are marks that indicate digging," he explained timidly. When he saw Rylee looking impressed, he spoke with a bit more authority. "I know because my uncle is in construction, and he showed me old plans he has in his house like this. Those are digging marks."

"Well," Bessie praised. "Aren't you the knowledgeable one?" She smiled at him and then noticed Rylee looked very proud of her new friend.

"OK," said Ben. "If Samuel is right, then this digging happened in several places. There are measurements on this document too. I think if we get a surveyor here, they could help us track down these spots."

"Brilliant," Bessie said. "I can't wait to see what you find." They each sat back in their chairs and smiled, wondering what secrets these possible tunnels could unearth. Samuel and Rylee sat smiling at one another, and Ginny was starting to get used to this behavior.

***

THE SUN SET as Samuel pulled down the blind across from where he and Rylee were sitting at the top of the south tower. There was a window on each of the four sides, so Samuel chose to close the one that faced other houses. It was unlikely that anyone would be looking up at them in the tower, but it made him feel they had at least a little privacy. He left the other three open because they had views of the harbor. There was a wicker love seat and two tiny tables sitting on either side of the tower, with the rest empty.

Rylee knew of no other place in Misty Bridge Bay she loved any more than the top of the spiral staircase. But tonight, she hardly noticed as all the historical information swirled through her mind. *It was so cool that Samuel helped by knowing what digging marks were. And were there really tunnels beneath this house or on our property?*

Samuel sat by her side, peeking in her direction from the corner of his eye. As a relatively new acquaintance, he was not confidently reading her facial expressions. "Are you alright?"

"Oh." She startled and faced him. "I guess so. It's just all this stuff. It's all so confusing and exciting and a little scary too."

"I know," he answered, only pretending not to think of only her. "Tunnels. Who could have guessed we would find tunnels?"

"Staircases, a hundred years of property owners, sheep and goats, and that little girl who couldn't walk well. There's so much involved in all of this. Sometimes, it overwhelms me when I think of it all." Her brow furrowed while he watched every movement of her face. With so many facts swirling around in her head, Rylee was unaware, of course.

"Elise Tuttle. So that was her name. I must say," he murmured. "Kind of a strange name."

She looked directly at him in a perplexed manner. "Strange?" she asked. "What do you mean by strange?"

"Oh," he said apologetically. "I mean, it's just not a name that you hear very often."

"Well, she lived here over a hundred years ago. Names change over time."

"That's true. I suppose Elise might have been a popular name back then."

Rylee started staring into space and took on a fierce pose again. "It's so sad. It would be horrible not to be able to walk." She paused and then continued. "In my dream, I was the little girl, so I have a little idea how it feels not to be able to lift one's legs. It's so awful."

"I guess it would be pretty hard," Samuel agreed. "How weird that you have dreamt you were her." Rylee looked at him in defense. "I don't mean that you are weird. It's the situation that's weird. You know?"

Rylee stood, lifted the blind slightly, and looked out across the bay. "I know what you meant. But Samuel," she said, "what I can't figure out is *why* I'm having that dream. I mean, until yesterday, I had never heard of Elise Tuttle before." She lifted her hands to her face in nervousness. "Samuel, how could I be dreaming of someone I never knew existed?" She turned to face him, twisting her hands around.

Samuel rose and gently took one of her hands in his. "I don't know how to answer that. I really don't know anything about the paranormal or ghosts or any of that stuff, but I'm sure we will figure it all out. Don't worry."

Rylee smiled. "Thank you for helping us. It all seems so crazy and scary. I'm so glad you're here."

They smiled at one another for what seemed like several minutes. A buzzing ringtone screeched from Samuel's pocket. He frowned and finally let her hand drop from his to reach for his cell phone. He turned off the ringer.

"It's my curfew," he said a bit meagerly. "I have to go, or I'll get grounded. I cannot get grounded just when things are getting interesting." *And I couldn't go without seeing you too.*

She smiled at his embarrassment. "I understand. I think my mom needs me to help her with some housework anyways. Better I think about cleaning than letting all this information jump around inside my head. If I do that, I will get and stay overwhelmed and scared, and that won't help anything."

He turned toward the stairs and retook her hand. "Walk me down?"

She managed a smile as they descended the spiral staircase together.

***

GINNY KEPT BUSY in the shop the rest of the week, knowing she had to wait a few days before talking to the surveyor. Focusing on her work was all she could do until then. Tourist after tourist came and went; however, one looked the same as the next, each day closing up and making the bank deposit a blur from one day to the next. Dinners with Rylee were mundane and quiet for the most part, each awaiting what would happen next.

"Have you had any of those dreams?" Ginny asked her daughter.

"Actually, no," answered Rylee in between bites. "But, I'm not expecting them to be gone just yet."

"How do you know? Maybe you won't have any more."

"I'm not getting my hopes up," answered the very young yet clever girl. "I used to think that way, only to be very disappointed when another one would come."

Ginny took empty dinner dishes to the sink to rinse. She turned. "It will be interesting to see what the surveyor tells us."

"How will he help, Mom?" Rylee looked at her mom with sleepy eyes.

"Well," said her mom. "He will help us look at the information we already have, add it to the information he has in his office, and give us his thoughts." She took in and let out a deep sigh. "In the end, I'm sure we'll end up looking for the tunnels," said Ginny.

"I can't believe all along there could be tunnels underground that we knew nothing about."

"I know," agreed Ginny with what Rylee looked to be a little fear in her eyes. "If there are tunnels, I'll need to figure out what to do to make them safe. I wouldn't want anyone mistakenly going down in them and getting stuck or lost."

"I never gave that a thought," said Rylee, staring into space.

"I can't help but wonder where they are."

"*If* they are there at all," Ginny reminded her daughter. "We don't know for sure they exist yet."

"Bessie seems to know what she's talking about," said Rylee. "My money's on us finding tunnels."

Ginny raised her eyebrows and continued to clear the table. Rylee helped with returning things to the refrigerator. Once Ginny wiped clean the table, she grabbed a book and retired to the living room. Rylee walked through on her way to her room and stopped short at the foot of the stairs.

"Mom, why would someone dig tunnels?" Rylee looked at her mother, quite perplexed.

"There could be many reasons. I guess we'll just have to wait and see." Ginny put down her book, sat upright, and thought to herself: *And who knows what we might find down there.* Ginny shivered at that thought.

***

Mr. Shepherd agreed to meet Ginny at her house that Friday

afternoon while Samuel and Rylee looked after the shop. They both stood in the back of the house, looking toward a wooded area not but 200 yards from their position. The surveyor held maps and looked over her property while he asked questions.

"So, according to what we have so far, I see the possibility of two tunnel outlets on your property."

"What do you mean by tunnel outlets?" asked Ginny.

"Most tunnels are not dead ends. For safety, it's best to have a second way out. It's hard to say where the tunnels start, but it might be easier to find where they come out."

"Oh," she said. "I see." She looked around from left to right, toward her property's edge. Mr. Shepherd scanned the property, with Ginny following as a mimic.

He looked at her with concern. "What I'm saying is that the tunnels probably originate…" He was then interrupted by a third party.

"Hello," came a very airy voice from behind as Ben walked up to join them. Ginny and the surveyor snapped their heads back, facing him. Ginny's face broke into a wide smile.

"Ben," said Ginny. "I'm glad you made it. Thanks for coming. "Mr. Shepherd was explaining that the best way to find tunnels is to find what he calls an outlet."

The surveyor opened up a chart he had brought from his office. "I have marked each possible outlet on this property and the properties connecting to the east and the west."

It was decided that the owners of the other two properties would be contacted, and when all were ready to search, a structural specialist would be involved. Ginny readily agreed, realizing it could be dangerous.

"How do we find these structural specialists?" asked Ben.

"Don't worry about that," answered Mr. Shepherd. "I'll be getting ahold of them. If you would like to talk to the neighbors, call me in the next couple of days. That will give me time to speak to the structural people. OK?"

"Of course," said Ginny, shaking his hand before he left. "Thank you so much for coming and for your guidance."

"My pleasure," he answered while shaking her hand. "This is a fascinating mystery to solve."

Ben and Ginny sat on an outside swing located in her backyard. As his legs were much longer than hers, he gently pushed, swaying back and forth. Ginny seemed to barely notice, deep in thought. He seemed to enjoy the silence as much as she; only his glance also indicated that he enjoyed looking at her as well.

"So much to take in," she said softly.

"I know." He breathed in deeply. "Maybe we should let our minds take a break from it, to take a rest."

She turned her head and smiled at him. Sighing, she also sat back against the swing.

"That's an excellent idea, a perfect idea." She paused for a moment and then continued. "I'll start contacting the neighbors tomorrow. Tonight, I'll just give it a rest."

They spent the rest of the night gently swinging and gazing at the stars. For the moment, that was exactly what each needed.

***

ONE WEEK LATER, the surveyor, Mr. Shepherd, stood at the very edge of what Ginny called her backyard with his back to the wooded area. Ten people stood around him in a semicircle, alert to his every word. To the side stood two prominent men in rugged, brown jumpsuits, work boots, and hard hats with lights ready for use. They each had quite a lot of large, thick rope draped over a shoulder with massive and strong-looking clasps one might expect a mountain climber to have. Ginny knew they were the structural specialists the surveyor had called. Ben stood slightly behind Ginny, and Rylee and Samuel were toward their left.

Ginny had secretly worried that some nosey villagers might sneak in to obtain juicy gossip to add to their nattering. Ginny looked all around and was relieved, seeing no one who would fit that description. The last thing she wanted to be known as was the lady with the spooky tunnels under her house and property. Mr. Shepherd spoke with authority.

"Now, as I said, these two men will search any possible opening we find first. If you find something suspicious, call out. Do not venture below the surface for any reason. Have I made myself clear?"

Silence fell over the small crowd as they nodded in agreement. Ben bent down and whispered in Ginny's ear. "He's talking to you too." Ginny looked at him, smiling and nodding.

"OK," said Mr. Shepherd. "As you can see, we are starting with Ginny's property. We will work till five o'clock, no later. More than likely, we will have to search the other two properties another day." The owners of those properties nodded in understanding. "You each have a detailed map of Ginny's property. Spread out in the directions indicated and call out if you find anything. Let's go!"

For an hour and a half, each group searched the property, making sure to stay relatively close to each other so each could hear a shout. Ben suggested to Samuel to walk a bit in front of Rylee in case the ground was to let loose underfoot. Rylee and Ginny each gave them stern looks at this proposition. Ben and Samuel quickly abandoned that topic.

Each group walked slowly, keeping their heads down, lifting branches from trees and wiry bushes that had grown out of control, many entangled with another. Much of Ginny's property had been wooded area. She only mowed a small portion around her house and shop. Ginny brushed a few strands of hair from in front of her eyes and kept looking.

Ben walked slightly over to Ginny's right, wanting to check

out a rather large grouping of overgrown bushes. At the same time, Mr. Shepherd and his two employed men did the same to Ginny's left. Ginny stopped and watched Ben as he walked around the perimeter of the overgrowth, lifting prickly limbs with his heavily protected arms and hands; all were instructed to wear thick workmen's jackets and gloves for this job.

"Anything?" asked Ginny.

"Not sure," answered Ben. Ginny started to step in his direction. "No, stay back. There's some poison ivy here." Ginny did as she instructed, not wanting to risk getting that unfortunate affliction.

At the same time, Mr. Shepherd and Ben both cried out. They each stood upright, looking at each other, unsure of how to proceed. Mr. Shepherd immediately took charge.

"We'll put a stake in the ground over here. Just stay there and wait for us to join you." Ben nodded.

Ginny shot an exciting look to Ben with her eyebrows raising toward her hairline. "Don't get your hopes up," he warned her. Ginny lowered her brows and nodded.

All those in the search party abandoned their posts and came to see what Ben had found. Ginny told each of them of the poison ivy, and all kept their distance except Samuel, who walked closer to Ben's position.

"Samuel!" Rylee cried out.

Samuel turned to her reassuringly. "It's alright. I'm naturally immune to it. I never get it even if I roll around in it."

Ginny and Rylee looked at each other with surprise while the guys lifted branches and mumbled to themselves. The only audible phrase was from Samuel. "Oh, I see what you mean."

As Mr. Shepherd and the two rugged men walked up to the intended spot, they asked Ben and Samuel to step aside once they had shown them the point of intrigue. It was hard to catch details as the three mumbled; however it eventually became known that a concrete corner had been discovered, peeking out from under the brush.

Mr. Shepherd turned and made an announcement. "It looks like it's going to take a little time to cut back all the growth before we see what this might be."

One of the two men walked back toward their pickup truck to get some tools, while the other made an effort to pull back as much of the shrubbery as he could. Mr. Shepherd looked at the small crowd as if he thought making his announcement would deter people from hanging around, but no one moved.

The second man returned from the truck with a gas-powered chain saw and, after putting on safety goggles, began to cut away the larger brush, too thick to pull away. Bits of wood and grass started flying out all around the saw, and some in the small group did step back a few paces. No one, however, wanted to miss seeing the discoveries. After removing the growth, a large, square-shaped concrete slab sat firmly above ground.

One of the men thoroughly examined its perimeter and stood up to share his findings. "It seems to be separated from a concrete base below. It's hard to say what's underneath." After some discussion, they decided to clear off the other location found using the chain saw.

The second location appeared to be a square-shaped structure, built above the ground, now completely covered in growth. It was made of large stones and mortar with four sides; one side appeared to be a door. It had an old, ring-shaped rusted handle, barely able to move.

"And to think that just looked like a bunch of bushes that had grown together," said Ginny. "It was so covered in growth, and the structure couldn't be seen. That's amazing."

"Sure is," agreed Rylee.

"That will be fun to try to open," said Mr. Shepherd to the other two men. "So, it's lunchtime. How about we break to eat and come back afterward and decide which one to tackle first?"

All agreed to this plan, and the small group dispersed, Mr. Shepherd and the two men heading to the nearest diner, the neighbors back to their houses, and the usual foursome back to Ginny's kitchen.

***

AN HOUR LATER, Mr. Shepherd looked pleased to see the onlookers from the adjacent properties were not present. Ginny, Ben, Rylee, and Samuel returned to the wooded location to find the three men had returned with a local man who owned an excavator. The front of the large equipment had an arm with a scoop with what looked like a giant metal thumb.

The four watched as the scoop scraped while pushing the heavy concrete slab to one side. Then, the thumb-shaped metal prong latched firmly over the top, allowing the slab to be lifted and moved off to the side of the grassy area. Anticipating their movements, Mr. Shepherd yelled out above the engine. "Don't move closer!" The four looked dejected as their plans squashed.

The job now completed, the driver of the heavy equipment backed away from the slab and turned off the engine. After jumping down, he joined the others standing off to the side, but as close as allowed.

Mr. Shepherd and the two structure specialists bent over to peer into the opening. Shining powerful flashlights downward, they were each quiet for some time. Ginny, losing patience, cried out.

"Well, what is it?" She eyed the three men with insistence.

Each of them stood upright, and Mr. Shepherd took a few steps toward Ginny while the structural specialists discussed the next moves quietly to themselves. Ginny and Ben walked forward to meet Mr. Shepherd.

"It's a set of old, stone steps. It goes down quite a ways,"

Mr. Shepherd explained.

Ginny gasped and started to move closer, but the surveyor stepped in front of her. "Larry and Mark," he said, looking back toward the rugged men now in the process of securing one end of a safety rope to a sturdy tree. "They will go down first. They will use their underground walkie-talkies to report back to us." Ginny looked concerned. "They've both done this kind of thing before. They are trained for this type of thing, and you, as the property owner, will be right there, listening to the reports with me."

Ginny looked at Ben, took a deep breath, and nodded in agreement. Ben put an arm around her and tried to hold her tightly in support. She smiled.

Paramedics were called and stood by their ambulance about 300 feet away, just on standby, as Mr. Shepherd explained. Somebody put up stakes with caution tape attached around the entire area to ensure all bystanders knew the limit.

Larry had descended the opening, securing a safety belt and rope around his waist. Behind the caution tape, Ginny broke Ben's hold, paced back and forth, her arms crossed before her torso. Ben watched her pace for some time before speaking to her.

"Ginny," he said, trying not to sound judgy. "What's going on with you?"

Ginny stopped pacing and walked up to him, and whispered. "It's just that…." She paused.

"It's just what?" asked Ben.

Ginny looked over at the opening and Mr. Shepherd and Larry. "It's just that anything could be down there." She looked at him. "Anything."

"Are you worried about something possibly being down there in particular?" he asked.

"No, of course not," she contended. "The idea of anything possibly being down there scares me."

He knew better than to take the conversation any further.

***

Reports starting coming through the communication device

Mr. Shepherd held, Larry busy handling the safety rope. Mark had reached the bottom of the steps after slipping down those crumpled and started to fall downward, caught by Larry above holding onto the safety rope.

Mark's voice crackled through the device. "I'm walking through a tunnel. The sides feel solid." There was a pause. "In some places, I can see stones and mortar sticking out. It's about 3.5 to 4 feet wide in most places, but I can feel that it narrows and widens from time to time."

Those listening from above were quiet, not wanting to miss any words coming from the device. Samuel and Rylee walked up closer beside Ginny and Ben. Samuel's cell phone began to ring, and he walked aside, told his father what was going on, and was relieved at having permission to stay.

Mark's voice continued to crackle. "The tunnel winds around corners. Not sharp corners, but rounded corners. The light on my hat isn't strong enough, so I'm turning on an extra flashlight." He spoke officially, most likely as trained.

It was quiet for three to four moments, and Ginny moved about restlessly, raising a hand to her face, one finger landing between her teeth. The small group had to wait several minutes before Mr. Shepherd broke the silence.

"Mark," he said. "Are you OK?"

Mark didn't readily answer, and a tense feeling washed over the entire group. Finally, their waiting ended.

"Yeah," Mark said. "I'm still here. I'm just surprised at how long this tunnel is." Pausing again before continuing. "It branched off in two directions. I followed one path, which led to what looked like an old, metal door. At least, I think it's a door. I backtracked and went the other direction, and that's the path I'm on now. It's like it keeps going on and on."

"Stay in communication," directed Mr. Shepherd.

"I will," answered Mark. The group could hear Mark breathing as he walked along the long and mysterious tunnel.

Ginny went back to pacing while Ben, Rylee, and Samuel stood together as still as statues. Mark made unimportant comments from time to time to make sure all above knew he was still safe and traveling along inside.

"OK," Mark said. Ginny's pacing stopped. A few seconds later, Mark explained. "In front of me is a set of stairs made of thick concrete. The walls also appear to have changed from stone and mortar to concrete. I'm preparing to ascend the stairs."

"Are you sure they are intact enough to be safe?" said Larry, surprising the group, who were only hearing his voice for the first time.

"I think so," answered Mark. "They are wide enough for me to move side to side, avoiding the broken and cracked steps. I'm beginning to ascend. They are curved. I have counted ten so far, and I'm still climbing."

Illustrated by: Rowan Wills

The afternoon sun was setting above ground, and Mr. Shepherd sent Samuel to his car to get a high-powered light. He returned as soon as he could, running all the way there and back.

"Mark?" Larry nearly yelled into the communication device."

"Yes," Mark answered. "After climbing twelve steps, I have hit a stop." A slight pause. "It looks like a door again. This one is different. A few feet before I got to the door, the concrete walls and steps turned into wood. The door looks like it's wood also. The earth above the door looks unstable. I will not open the door by myself at this time."

"No," shouted Larry and Mr. Shepherd simultaneously. Mr. Shepherd continued on his own. "You're right. Leave the door alone."

"I think I should come back," said Mark. "I'm heading back now."

"OK," said Mr. Shepherd. "Easy going."

Larry looked at Mr. Shepherd. "Two doors, huh?"

As Mark was pulled from the underground opening, he immediately reached for a water bottle. He rested, leaning against a large, stable tree that proved durable enough for his safety harness and rope. Larry and Mr. Shepherd were on either side, and Ginny was asked to join them. Ben stayed back, waiting with Rylee and Samuel.

After their discussion ended, Ginny returned to the others and shared what she had learned. "Mark had a video recorder on him because GPS stopped working when he got so far down underground."

"That was clever of them," said Rylee smiling.

"Very," answered her mom. "They are going to take his recording and watch it with a map while attempting to plot out his journey. They think that will give them a better idea of where the doors might be. They're done for tonight. They plan to keep a police car here all night to make sure no one bothers the opening."

The four of them turned and walked back to the house. Ben returned to his sister's house, and Samuel headed back before his father got mad and grounded him. Rylee and her mom spent a quiet night at home. Rylee decided not to go to the tower to read that night. There was too much to think about now, and she wanted to stay closer to her mom.

***

The next day, Mr. Shepherd called early and asked if Ginny would have time to talk about their findings later that day. Ginny set up an appointment time after she closed up the shop. Ben had told her earlier he had to attend a virtual meeting in the afternoon. Not wanting to cause too much confusion for him, Ginny decided not to bother him about her appointment and instead went to Mr. Shepherd's office alone.

She closed up shop, walked down to the bank to drop off the daily deposit, and then over two blocks to the surveyor's office. It had been a dreary day, and Ginny walked along the sidewalk past several Victorian homes slightly smaller than her own and around a corner and up a set of porch steps.

Mr. Shepherd's house held his surveying office within as well. This was a trend in Misty Bridge Bay. Ginny walked to the end of the porch and knocked on a door, a rather smart-looking engraved plaque hanging to its side. Once inside, she sat opposite the surveyor, poised behind a rather large oak desk. He had a map outstretched between them, pointing to various locations and marks.

Ginny listened intently, most of the time with her mouth hanging open wide. Outside, the afternoon grew darker and darker, and once the meeting was complete, she rose, shook hands, and began her short walk back home. All the while, Mr. Shepherd's last words repeated over and over in her head. *For now, it's best you and I just keep this between the two of us.*

Ginny didn't have to explain anything to Rylee, as she had made plans to stay at a friend's house before Mr. Shepherd's call. No one knew she had this meeting; no one needed to know, at least not yet.

The coming week led to many exciting events. A crew was engaged in digging in front of the metal door, taking away danger for a crew member working on getting on the other side of the door. This crew was hard at work quite a distance from Ginny's house. News had blazed through the town like wildfire. All eyes were upon this endeavor. Each day, people showed up to observe the progress, which was slower than anyone expected. Thankfully, people typically ended up getting bored and leaving.

Workers exposed the tunnel and the metal door, which required a blow torch and other tools to open. Ginny, Ben, Rylee, and Samuel were back to examine the find. Upon opening the door, Larry reported finding barrels of what he assumed was some type of alcohol, a very dusty easy chair, and a rather large safe.

Mr. Shepherd identified the safe as being from the early 1900s, with some difficulty to break. Other workers were called in to break open the safe and further identify and confirm the barrels' contents. Mr. Shepherd, Larry, and Mark were not needed for this.

Ben and Ginny stood off to the side and watched for a while. "So, what do they think about this? Hiding hooch?" Ben laughed. "Why a safe? And who was hiding this?" Ben didn't wait for any answers in between questions.

"No one knows, Ben," answered Ginny.

Her tone concerned him. "Is there something else on your mind?"

Ginny nodded and told him to follow her back to her house. Once there, she explained that Mr. Shepherd, Larry, and Mark were not working on a different property as previously announced. She went on to explain that they were working on finding where the other path of the tunnel led.

"Why does that need to be such a secret?" he asked her in response to her whispers.

"They didn't want everyone to know that they think it comes out under my house."

"Really?"

"Really," she repeated. "They think it might be unsafe for people outside the family to know."

"I would agree," he sternly said.

As she walked into her house, she stopped in the kitchen at the door to the basement while Ben followed. They both walked down the steps into the dark, dust-filled basement. Ginny chose not to use the basement because she had plenty of storage space otherwise.

"I asked him where in the basement he thought it led to, and you know what he said?"

Ben shook his head. "What did he say?"

"He said it didn't lead to the basement." She let her hands

slap her jeans. "Not in the basement. Why wouldn't it lead to the basement?"

"I don't know," answered Ben. "Maybe because it would be too obvious?" He looked around but saw no sign of an opening. "They must be right."

Ginny walked up the stairs back to the kitchen as Ben followed again. Ginny shut the basement door and pulled the lock as she usually would.

"Then where did he say it came out?" Ben was way too impatient to wait any longer.

At that point, Rylee descended the stairs of the south tower, carrying a book and a small blanket. She set them down and walked into the parlor, joining Ben and Ginny.

"What's going on?" she asked them. "What are you talking about?"

Ginny took a deep breath and explained it all to her daughter.

"Wait a minute," she said. "Where did he think it came out?"

"She was about to tell me," said Ben.

***

That evening, Rylee and Ginny decided to sleep in the living room. Ginny locked the front doors and the lock on the door from the living room to the parlor Ginny had Ben install earlier that day. Each found their spot on two large couches and made their beds. Leaning back on pillows, Rylee and her mother each dove into a book. Ben wanted to spend the night in the house, but Ginny refused, stating she and her daughter would be fine.

Rylee looked up from her book and sent a slightly scared look in her mom's direction. Mom smiled back at her. "Just one night," reassured Ginny. Rylee smiled, nodded, and returned her nose to her book. Ginny looked up, noticing the police car slowly patrolling past her house.

Outside and without Ginny knowing, Ben walked into the glow of the streetlight to show who he was and waved to the officers posted at both tunnel opening locations. Each officer waved back, showing they knew who he was and allowing him to proceed closer. He walked over to the opening most immediate to Ginny's backyard.

"Sir," said the officer. "I know why you are here, but you are not allowed to be here."

Illustrated by: Alexis Mamula

"I know," said Ben. "I just couldn't sit at home knowing

someone could get into the tunnel and maybe find their way into Ginny's house." Ben looked over toward the Victorian home. "Can I get you guys some coffee?"

At that moment, the other officer from deeper within the woods spoke over the radio, typically clipped on the belt. "Jamison," said the other officer. "Ben has to leave."

"That's what I told him," answered Jamison. Then he looked back at Ben. "We don't need coffee, Ben. We're being relieved by other officers in one hour."

Ben looked back to Ginny's house and put his hands into his jean pockets. Officer Jamison was as gentle as he could be. "Goodbye, Ben." The officer smiled at him.

Ben nodded, smiled, and started walking back toward the streetlight. He turned back around and spoke. "Keep them safe." Reluctantly, he walked back to his sister's house.

The next day, Mr. Shepherd pulled up to Ginny's house. He was met at the door by Rylee and entered the dining room to a nearly full table. Ginny, Ben, and Samuel were seated, and when Rylee and their guest took their seats, the table was full.

Mr. Shepherd set a briefcase on the table before him and

began to speak. "Ginny, starting today, people from the national and local historical society will be coming to take pictures of the tunnel. I have provided all the information they need to record this find properly. After they leave, I strongly suggest you allow us to fill in the tunnel outlets. I don't see how you and your daughter can be safe as long as they are open."

"Safe?" asked Samuel.

Mr. Shepherd rose and took them all to the parlor. "We discovered the location of the entrance to the tunnel." He addressed Ginny. "OK if those present know of this location?"

She nodded. As they all stood in silence, Mr. Shepherd lifted his hand toward the fireplace mantel. He then took three steps to the right and removed a few books from the massive bookshelves built in on either side of the fireplace.

"I have taken all those books off these shelves and cleaned. There's nothing back there." Ginny walked closer to Mr. Shepherd.

"There is this little hole," he answered as she leaned in to see as he pointed.

"Well, yes, there's always been a hole there, but—"

At that moment, Mr. Shepherd poked the hole with his pointer, and the whole group heard a loud click. Ginny gasped. At that moment, the same bookshelf snapped away from the wall. Ginny moved back slightly as the surveyor grabbed hold of the bookshelf and pivoted it open like a door.

Samuel jumped over the back of the couch, landing on the cushions to get a better view as the rest leaned in as close as possible, peering behind the bookshelf.

"As you can see, there's a very steep and curved stairway that leads to the tunnels below. At the bottom, we found the steps Mark originally found that first day he entered the tunnel."

Ginny crossed her arms and shivered as a distinct coldness escaped from the tunnel entrance into the parlor. Mr. Shepherd understood and pushed the bookcase closed again and returned the books to their place on the shelves.

He turned to the group. "Shall we return to the dining room?"

After they took their seats once again, Mr. Shepherd continued to explain. "Ginny, someone who owned your house many, many years ago dug these tunnels. They made the other way out that we found under the concrete slab."

"How would they have ever gotten out of the tunnel there?" Ben asked. "It took heavy equipment to move that slab to open it."

"Good question," answered the surveyor. "After we looked at it a bit closer, we determined that the slab was not the original cover. We found an indentation in the concrete around the opening that there used to be some type of hinges, which we think were attached to some kind of metal covering."

"I see," said Ben. "So, someone decided to cover the tunnel opening for good and used a heavy concrete slab to do it."

"Right," answered Mr. Shepherd.

Ginny asked the most important question of all. "So, someone was hiding something down in that other room inside the safe, right?"

Mr. Shepherd pulled out what looked to be a filthy, dusty journal book, safely inside a sealed plastic bag. "It was all written in this diary. It doesn't say who the writer is, but it makes one thing very clear."

"What's that?"

Mr. Shepherd looked past the others, directly to Rylee. "Your mother told me of the dream that you have had several times."

Rylee didn't speak. "The writer in this book states clearly that the brother of Elise Tuttle—the little girl who couldn't walk—whom he gladly carried up to her favorite place at the top of the south tower—was hit by a car driven by someone the writer names." Everyone waited in expectation.

"Wait a minute," Samuel chimed in. "Were there even cars back in those days? Didn't everyone still use horse-drawn carriages?"

"Excellent question," said Mr. Shepherd. "The car was very new. Only a few rich people had them. A boy named Rich Dryer was driving a car back to its owner. The book explains that Elise's brother bulleted his bike out into the road from a path in the woods on a back road. Rich Dryer and Elise were in love with each other. That made it all the more terrible."

"Oh no," sighed Rylee. "The car hit the bike or vice versa."

"That's right," agreed Mr. Shepherd. "The writer of this book saw it happen and took pity on the boy. He agreed not to tell anyone, and he helped him cover it all up."

"I can't believe that boy could keep such a secret to himself," said Samuel.

"He didn't," explained Mr. Shepherd. "He ended up telling Elise the truth before he died."

"Before he died?" asked Ginny.

"He became sick, and the doctors couldn't help him. The book didn't describe what he had, but it said that he told Elise the truth."

"I can't imagine how she might have felt," said Ginny.

"We don't have to imagine," answered the surveyor. "The book says that she immediately forgave him and would never divulge it."

"My dream," sighed Rylee. "All this, and we still didn't find any reason for my dream." Rylee's head lowered to the table as her mom covered her daughter's hand with her own.

"Rylee," Mr. Shepherd said quietly with empathy. "I think I might have discovered something to do with that too."

Ginny and Rylee spun their heads in his direction. He had everyone's attention still.

"The writer explained that in remembrance of her brother and the boy whom she loved, she struggled up to the top of the tower every night to light two candles in the windows. Then, she did it again to blow them out before going to bed. Eventually, the rest of her family started going up to do it for her, but she still made sure it happened every night."

Rylee looked at her mom. "That could be it. Could we?"

Her mother interrupted her. "We'll get electric candles and put them on a timer. One for each of them."

Rylee smiled while everyone else sat quietly, just taking it all in.

"I have a feeling that my dreams will be a little different now," said Rylee.

***

THAT NIGHT, she and her mother set electric candles in two windows and put them on a timer to go on each night and off each morning. Rylee still sat in the tower to read, sometimes just to sit. Night after night, there she sat, totally unafraid, knowing all too well that Elise was sitting right there beside her side, no longer worrying about lighting the candles. And there were no more dreams.

SCARY MARY

SCARY MARY

"Well, whatever you do, don't push Scary Mary too far," said the regional director. "The last thing we need is blood dripping down our walls." She then smiled, chuckled under her breath, and turned and walked out of the building, having completed her monthly departmental visit.

None of the workers guessed how true this prediction would become in just a few short weeks.

***

Donna pulled keys from her purse and let herself into the first and second locked doors at the 300 Downy Garden Drive basement office. Seven o'clock in the morning was early, but she found it the best time to get work done. It was peaceful, quiet, and no phones ringing one call after another.

She walked back to her office, opening the combination lock on her door with four numbers. She turned on the lights and prepared to sit down at her computer, remembering the two reports and early meeting on her schedule for the day. After hanging her jacket over her desk chair, a familiar thought entered her mind. *I couldn't be more thirsty.*

Donna grabbed her favorite glass and headed out to a room with a small kitchen, including a water cooler. After filling her cup, she ran her fingers through her thick blonde hair, exited the kitchen room, and turned left and down the hall to return to her small office. But, before getting there, she stopped abruptly upon hearing a strange sound. *What was that?*

Standing still, she took a sip of water and shrugged her shoulders, assuming the noise came from an office above. They were always loud in the upstairs office. Sometimes, it sounded like a bunch of wild animals walking across the floor. They often referred to them as The Zoo. And as luck would have it, the loud noises seemed always to come when they needed silence. Before taking any additional steps, the noise repeated. *Swoop, followed by a thud!*

Donna swallowed hard as she turned around and started walking toward Julia's front office, from where she thought the noises came. Only a few steps away, she found herself standing in front of the front office door, looking through a narrow window. Everything looked quiet and calm, as far as she could see.

She set her water glass on top of a shred box and pushed buttons on the combination code, different from the one on her office door. Darkness was all she saw as she peered through a small window in the door into the small receptionist area. The green light on the lock indicated that it had unlocked, allowing her to open the door and slowly step in.

The sounds she heard were familiar to her. *Swoop and thud* was the sound made by a desk drawer opening and closing. Four workers in that office day after day, with several drawers, opening and shutting, meant she couldn't be mistaken about the source of the sound. *That was a drawer!* There was no doubt in her mind. But, after switching the light on, she saw that none of the drawers were open.

She looked from one side of the room to the other, realizing this was another unexplained event in the office. In the past five months, several unexplained noises, doors opening and closing, moving objects, and several other unexplained events had occurred. *Here we go again.*

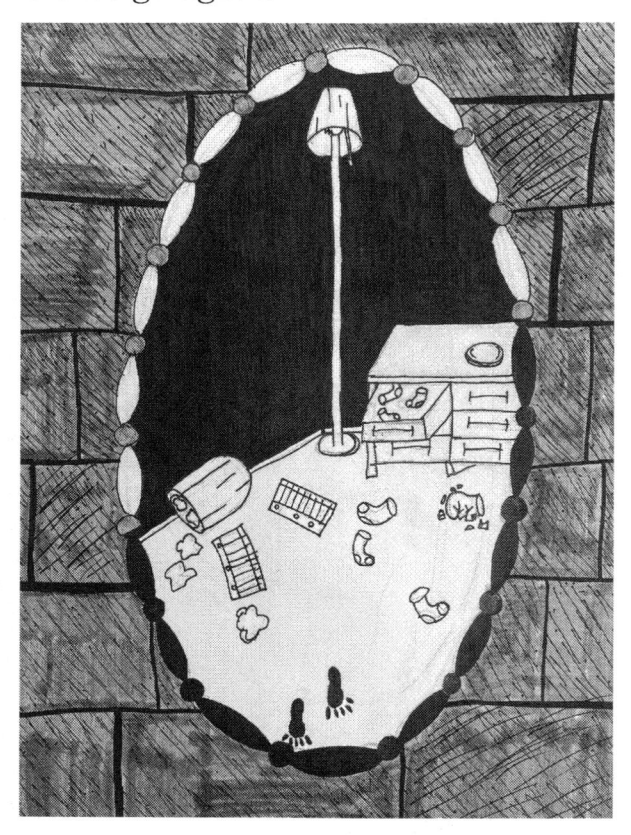

Illustrated by: Ashton Carlisle

She rolled her eyes and returned to her office, determined to finish those reports before the scheduled meeting. A little background music helped drown out any leftover fears or noises. *Ain't no one got time for this.*

Three hundred Downy Garden Drive sat on the back of a horseshoe-shaped road, which spun off a busy boulevard, boasting every type of fast food option one could desire. The building was made of sturdy, brown brick and had several doors leading to the outside, closed by security each night. It was a brisk and slightly windy fall day. Office personnel could be seen busily walking toward their places of employment, donned in overcoats and light sweaters. The chill in the air was a warning of the cold winter yet to come. The coolness felt inside the basement office was an entirely different one altogether.

Later that morning, Donna was joined by Pammy, Carly, and Julia. Clients to call and contracts to complete made for a hectic day. After her virtual meeting, Donna opened a door and joined her team in the front office, located down the hall.

"Good morning," she said to each of them as they busily faxed, documented, or hung up the phone. Each reciprocated her greeting. "Well," she continued, "had another one of those strange events again this morning."

They each stopped their work, turned to face her with eyes wide and jaws dropped. No one spoke. They were both afraid and excited to hear at the same time.

"What happened?" asked Julia.

"I was in my office a little after seven trying to get these reports done. I got some water from the conference room, and when I was walking back, I heard a drawer open and close," explained Donna as she held several papers in her hand.

"Really?" asked Carly. "What room did it come from?"

Donna smiled. "You're all sitting in it."

Immediately, they each peered with wide eyes at the many desk drawers in the small front office. One by one, with uncertainty in their eyes, Pammy and Carly each returned to their offices. Suddenly, that room didn't feel quite as cozy as it did a few minutes ago.

Julia turned around in her chair to face Donna. "This is getting creepy now."

"Getting?" asked Donna.

***

Pammy was the first to be hired in the department. After Carly joined, it didn't take long for trust to develop. Pammy told Carly of some strange happenings years ago that didn't quite fit in with the rest. Carly thought otherwise.

"A snake outside the furnace room? A wolf spider in the conference room?" said Carly, yelling down the hall from her office chair. "Those two events have to be related to the others, Pammy. How could a snake and a spider of that size get all the way down in this office?"

Pammy walked from her office to Carly's doorway. "No," she said. "The spider came in on a wheelchair, and the maintenance men said the snake had crawled up through a drain in the furnace room that was missing a cover." Carly sighed in disbelief. "I'm telling you," continued Pammy. "Both of those events had reasonable explanations."

"If you say so," said Carly as she resumed typing on her computer.

"I know there's something creepy going on in this office, but

I don't think the spider and snake have anything to do with it." Pammy returned to her office to work, sat down, and wondered. Carly was right about so many things. Could this be one of them?

***

Two days later, Julia walked down the back hall toward the restroom. She reminded the others of client appointments scheduled over the next two days on her way down the hall. Donna, Pammy, and Carly continued to discuss business matters. Julia came out of the bathroom and turned to the left to head back to the lunchroom.

Startled, she stopped several feet short of the lunchroom and stared at the door to an empty office. She didn't speak. She only stared. After drumming up some courage, she raised her voice over the others and asked a question. "Who was in this office?"

Each of the three joined her, fully knowing her voice sounded odd. Julia still stared at a slightly open door with a dark office behind. Donna moved closer to the other three to have a better view.

Julia turned around, looked at the other three, and repeated the question. "Were any of you in this office recently?" None of them answered. They only looked at each other while each shook their head no.

The empty office had sat vacant for months or maybe closer to a year. All it contained was extra furniture not currently used. There was absolutely no reason for anyone to need to enter that room.

"Oh, come on," whined Julia. "One of you had to have gone into that office, right? That door was closed when I came in this morning." Julia looked back at the ajar door, and after a few seconds of silence, they each returned to their work. No one wanted to talk about it any further.

***

EXCITEMENT SPREAD through the building when they heard they were getting a new neighbor in the office next door. They used the adjacent office for various reasons before being filled. Now that someone had taken the office suite, this couldn't happen anymore. Julia kept the adjoining door key in her top desk drawer.

Very late one afternoon, the staff left except for Pammy and Carly. The two sat in the front office, finishing up some last-minute work. They chatted and joked pleasantly, unaware of anything until the chatting ceased. They looked at each other in fear as they listened to the sound of a key thrusting into the lock of the adjacent office door.

"Did you hear that?" asked Carly.

Before Pammy could answer, the scratching sound resumed. They each gasped.

After about thirty seconds, the sound stopped. Frozen at first, Pammy rose and quietly stepped out from the receptionist area, past the shred box, and peeked around the corner at the door. She saw and heard no one, but she sure felt shaken.

"Anything?" asked Carly.

Pammy shook her head in disagreement.

"So, is the door still locked?" asked Carly.

"I guess so," answered Pammy.

Carly made a snapping sound with her mouth, slightly making fun of Pammy's fear and apprehension. "So, check and see," she dared.

Pammy gripped her lower lip with her upper teeth and somehow drummed up the courage to check the lock. Her hand shook and shivered on its way to the doorknob. Halfway there, it stopped, and Pammy took a deep breath, hoping to carry on. She took another wary step forward and let her trembling hand reach the knob. It didn't turn no matter how hard she tried.

They both sighed in relief. "It's locked."

Carly smiled. "That's good." When Pammy didn't return to the front office right away, Carly had an idea. "Something must have just scratched up against the door. Who knows what they could be doing over there."

"That's true," agreed Pammy. "Well, I think I'm getting out of here."

They clocked out and headed out the front office doors within two minutes. Pammy looked in the direction of the new office door only a few feet down the hall. "Wait a minute, Carly."

"Why?" she asked. "What is it?"

Pammy walked nearer to the new tenant's door. "There are

no lights on. There isn't anyone in there." Carly walked closer to see for herself. "It's only been two minutes at the most since we heard the sound at the door. If it wasn't the staff, who—or what—was it?"

***

THE OFFICE BUILDING in question had a primary and lower level floor. The basement floor housed three offices, whereas the upper level had two occupied offices. Donna, Julia, Pammy, and Carly worked in the middle of the three lower-level offices. With offices on both sides and above, it wasn't uncommon to hear strange noises coming from all sides.

When Pammy and Carly needed quiet to concentrate, it seemed the offices above insisted that it was time to do the vacuuming. Angry vacuuming is what they called it because every push of the sweeper followed with a loud thud of it hitting into the furniture of some sort. They could hear water or some liquid at certain times of the day, rushing down through pipes inside the outer office walls. Strange noises were a typical occurrence in their office.

During a jam-packed Thursday afternoon, appointments had been back to back for Pammy. Donna returned phone calls, completed intakes, and attended management meetings most of the day. Pammy and Donna were nowhere to be found between nine and one o'clock, each consumed with work. It was Carly's day off. Julia answered so many phone calls that her right ear was starting to feel sensitive and sore. Julia only spoke to Donna a few times when she forwarded a few calls back to her.

After Pammy finished up with her last client in the large conference room, she opened the hall door, as the room was stuffy. While she returned chairs to their tables, she heard Julia cry out.

"Who locked this file cabinet?"

"You mean the main one?" asked Pammy. "Why would anyone lock it in the middle of the day?"

Julia was now in the hall, Pammy under the hall threshold, and Donna walked out of her office and toward them while smoothing down her top. It was hard to decide whose eyes were bulged the biggest.

"You mean you just found the central filing cabinet locked?" asked Donna, wanting to make sure what she heard.

"Yes," answered Julia. "The key is safely inside my top drawer as usual." She paused, and no one spoke before she. "I *never* left my desk all day. I didn't bring lunch, so I sat there, nibbling at the snack basket that the marketer brought the other day."

Donna nodded. Pammy looked from one to the other and then broke the uncomfortable silence.

"Well, you both know I was in here all day," she said, pointing back inside the conference room. "Anyways, locking it in the middle of the day would be ridiculous. None of us would do that."

"Guess it was our friend again," said Donna, turning up the corners of her mouth.

Pammy and Julia didn't have anything intelligent to add, so they turned on their heels and returned to their tasks. It was easier to think of it as a joke.

Silence fell on the office for the next several weeks. Clients came and went without any sign of the mischievous office spirit. For most workers, this meant time to focus on their work. For Pammy, it meant time for research.

***

AFTER TWO RINGS, the regional director answered her phone. With only a few minutes until the next meeting, Pammy wasted no time asking for information. Her director was quite confused.

"I don't understand," asked the busy director. "You want to know who the old cleaning lady was?"

"Yes," answered Pammy. "I would like her name and the service that employs her."

After several uncomfortable, silent seconds, she provided the information requested.

One quick call resulted in hearing Tammy, the previous cleaning lady, explain that she had asked her boss to change her post. "I felt creeped out; that's all, just creeped out."

"Turns out," Pammy told Donna, "she couldn't explain why she felt scared. She was so frightened that she lied to her boss, saying that she had to change her schedule. She was so glad when her boss didn't question her further."

"Well," Donna nodded, "that new cleaning lady doesn't seem to notice anything."

Pammy grinned. "As far as we know, that is."

Pammy was conveniently last out from the office that night, knowing it was the cleaning lady's night. While making copies, just to find something to do to kill time, Pammy heard the back door open. Realizing this was the cleaning lady, Pammy grabbed the documents from the machine and made her way back to her office, just in time to be at her desk before the cleaning cart started rolling down the hall.

"Oh, hello," said Pammy to Cindy as she walked past her office door. As usual, Cindy was quite pleasant.

"Oh, I didn't see you there," answered Cindy.

"I'll be out of your way very quickly," Pammy said as she stood at her desk and gathered her bags.

"Oh, that's OK," said Cindy. "Has everything been alright?"

"Oh yes," said Pammy, slipping an arm into her coat. "Everything has been fine."

Pammy followed the cleaning lady and the cart down the hall on her way out of the office. Right before she turned toward the door, she paused and faced Cindy.

"Sure can be creepy down here at night all by yourself. I've been here at night working, and it definitely felt a bit scary to me."

Cindy moved toward the door where Pammy stood. "I supposed it could be. But, I'm so used to cleaning old buildings at night that I don't notice anymore. Old buildings settle and make weird noises. I used to clean stuffy museums and old three-story banks made of stone. Those were really creepy at first. After a while, you just don't notice anymore."

"You are brave. Well, have a good night," said Pammy as she left for home. She hated to admit it to herself, but she was a bit disappointed with Cindy's answer.

It was time to look into the property's history, hoping to find clues explaining all the strange happenings.

***

Pammy emailed anyone she thought might know anything

about the history of the office property. Finally, after a few days, she received a return email from Damon in marketing. After giving him some time to dig up some information, he gave her plenty to consider.

It was after hours, not that she would know, having gotten used to there being no windows. She became lost among the details in the emails. Hours passed by, and still, she read. She read about many families who lived on the property before, and then one, in particular, caught her eye.

Louisa Sharpe lived in a two-story home with her two brothers and parents, who were very wealthy. Apparently, they spread their wealth around very generously. Schools, the local hospital, and charity organizations benefitted from their help. Louisa was the youngest of the Sharpe children.

Mary and Thomas Sharpe stayed busy raising funds while their older children made the headlines for less than impressive reasons, such as misbehaving in clubs. On the other hand, Louisa seemed to remain out of trouble. Pammy laughed while reading articles of the brothers' antics and began to feel sorry for the parents, who seemed only to want to help the community.

A crash sound rang throughout the once silent office without warning, making Pammy jump. Shaking throughout the core of her body, she walked through the long hallway, carrying the only weapon available to her, in the form of a three-hole punch. Shaking, she held it above her head and crept toward the main conference room.

Slowly turning the doorknob and opening the door, she peered inside. Nothing seemed to be amiss. As she walked toward the small kitchen counter, something crunched under her shoes. She stopped and looked down, lifting her shoe to see what was underneath. It was fragments of a drinking glass. She looked up at a cupboard door that hung open and wondered how this could have happened. Surely she would have noticed this as she walked past this area on her way into the office.

"Scary Mary, please stop playing your tricks," she said out loud. She blew her blonde hair from in front of her eyes, lowered the hole punch, and walked back to her office, angry at having been interrupted. Not to mention her upper back muscles, already injured, sore from holding up her weapon.

Lost in reading, she rubbed her eyes and glanced at the

clock, wondering the time. She moaned at the late hour, hit print, and grabbed her belongings, deciding to take the copies home to finish. Turning off her office lights, she shut the door and walked to the other end of the hall, to the front office.

At first glance, no papers laid in the tray, despite being sure she heard the printer working. Like the apparition, Scary Mary, Pammy also named the copier Roger. As often as she yelled at it in frustration, she figured it needed a name. Unfortunately, he got yelled at too this time.

"Great," she yelled. "Now Roger and Scary Mary are working together against us." She sighed, marched back to her office to try printing again, and returned to the front office to retrieve the much-needed information.

Once grabbing the copies, she yawned, locked the front office door, heading to the main entrance. Frozen in fear, she furrowed her brows at the surprise of hearing what sounded like thunder, followed by earthquake-like shaking. She had to grab the walls to brace herself and keep from falling. No one in a basement office would hear or feel thunder down this far underground, and the likelihood of an earthquake in this part of the country was a lot less.

Pammy's statuesque stance was interrupted by shaking walls, drawers violently opening, spilling out contents, and lights blinking overhead. Afraid of losing the papers, she shoved them into a bag and began to attempt to walk. Holding on to the walls and stumbling, all the while sure the entire building was about to collapse, she screamed for help. No one heard. She knew no one heard.

Illustrated by: Ashlyn Alberts

She was her only hope to get out. Tears flew out of her eyes, and yet she plowed on. She didn't have much choice. Dropping and picking up her bag several times, she refused to leave without the papers. Scary Mary dearly wished to prevent her from leaving the office. The wind rushed through the rooms as if she was outside, and Pammy struggled against it toward the doors.

She finally made her way there and reached for the door, turning the doorknob with all the strength she had left. It turned, and she jumped through into a small lobby. Not stopping, she grabbed the final door into the hallway, her body sucked through the narrow opening, the door slamming shut, no doubt as a result of the strong winds.

Her body fell to the hallway floor, her bag and other belongings toppled on top of her. Exhausted, Pammy gasped for air and slowly looked along the long hall, quiet and desolate as usual for this time of the evening. She rose to her feet before anyone noticed her disheveled condition. The elevator bell rang, and she looked back at the office door, wondering if that storm indoors really did just happen or if it was all in her mind.

She sprinted up the back stairs and out of the building, walking toward her car. As she stepped off the curb, a security car startled her, stopping in front of her. A young security guard trying to look cool in sunglasses looked up at her.

"You alright, ma'am?" he asked.

"Yes," she said, trying to be convincing. "Yes, I am. Thank you." Pammy walked around the car and dashed into hers. It was time to discover what Scary Mary didn't want her to know. *And on top of that, I'm getting too old for this kind of crap.*

***

THE NEXT DAY, the office looked and ran as usual with nothing out of place and no sign of the events of the previous evening. Pammy walked in with a stunned and almost peaceful attitude. She walked into the front office, remarking on the fully intact walls without cracks or signs of the internal storm. Slowly she walked into the front office, where Julia, Carly, and Donna sat talking about the day's business ahead.

Noticing her blank stare, they stopped talking. Donna stood up, walked to her, and checked on her.

"Pammy," she said gently. "Are you alright?"

Pammy looked up and snickered. "That's the same question

the security officer asked me last night."

"Last night?" asked Carly.

"Why don't you sit down where I was sitting," Donna offered. Pammy complied.

"What's going on?" asked Julia.

Pammy looked at each of them, trying to decide where to begin, wondering if they would believe her if she told them what she experienced in this office the previous evening. She decided to skip it and move on.

"I got an email from Damon in marketing," she started. "There was so much information that I decided to print it off and take it home to read it."

"Last night?" asked Donna.

Pammy looked up at her, wondering if she could tell that she wasn't coming clean about what happened there last night. It didn't matter.

"We had it all wrong," Pammy said. "All wrong."

Carly joined in. "What was it that we had all wrong?"

Pammy looked around the room and saw closed drawers; nothing spilled on the floor and no sign of the terrifying storm of the previous night. Looking back at her coworkers, she continued.

"It's not Mary. All the time, it was Louisa. Louisa Sharpe has been here with us."

"Look," said Julia while running her hands through her layered hair. "Don't tell me there are two ghosts in this place. I can barely handle one."

Pammy smiled. "No, there's only one, and her name is Louisa."

Donna looked at Julia. "Cancel everything we had scheduled this morning. I have a feeling this is a story we need to hear." Pammy smiled even wider than before.

They sat around a conference table waiting to hear the full story in the conference room, drinks all around. Pammy took a very long gulp of water, a deep breath afterward, and then braced herself to share everything.

"I know we have been teasingly calling our resident spirit Scary Mary, but I think it's actually a very sweet, young girl named Louisa Sharpe. We have been blaming her for all the crazy stuff happening around here. And, I'm sure she hasn't liked the name either. We've been talking so badly about her, and it's no wonder she's been playing tricks on us and making a nuisance of herself. That's on me since I named her."

No one interrupted her. She wouldn't have noticed if they had and hammered on. "A very long time ago, there was this very influential family named Sharpe. The mother and father were very wealthy when they settled in our town. They were all about helping the community. They gave all kinds of money for a church and school and raised lots of money for various charities. As far as I can tell from the information I have, everybody liked them. Well, everybody liked the parents and the youngest daughter named Louisa."

"Youngest?" Carly asked. "So they had other kids too?"

"Yep," Pammy said, smiling at her. Then she looked down at her glass of water and continued to share. "They also had two boys who were older than Louisa. They were trouble. From what I gather, they were wild, rude, and nothing but town troublemakers. Damon said that everything he had on them said the rest of the family were ashamed of their behavior."

"Well," explained Pammy. "That was all I read before I realized how late it was, so I printed the rest of it off, and…took it home to read."

Donna, Julia, and Carly looked suspiciously at Pammy. Pammy rushed on, avoiding a question she didn't want to answer.

"After I got home, I read the rest, and it said that Louisa died when she was very young of some accident. It didn't specify how but she died very young. It said that she wanted so badly to help her parents with their community charitable work but that she died before she was old enough. The parents were devastated, and after a few years, their health failed, and they also died, leaving half their wealth to charities and the other half to their rowdy sons."

"I think I know what happened next," said Julia. "They blew the money; end of the story."

"No," corrected Pammy. "That's not the end of the story. You see, her brothers did sell everything off, took loads of money, and ran off to live in some exclusive part of the world."

"Like I said," Julia asserted. "They blew all the money."

"Well, on second thought, you're probably right about that," said Pammy. "But, that's not the important part. You see, after that, people said they could see Louisa's ghost walking throughout the community, watching when new buildings were being built, and standing off to the side smiling at charity events. They say she watches all the events that she would have liked to attend and support but never had the chance to."

"So, what does any of that have to do with us?" asked Julia.

Donna gasped. "I get it," she said. "Our building went up soon after she died?"

"Yes, but it's more than that," said Pammy. "Our building… our department, is built right on the same land the Sharpes' old Victorian mansion once stood."

"Wait a minute," interrupted Carly. "Why in the world would the historical society allow what was sure to be a beautiful old mansion to be torn down?"

"They didn't have a choice," explained Pammy. "The boys sold the land for top dollar to a big developing company. They didn't care about their family home, and so down it came."

"And up went office buildings. Oh my golly," said Donna with her jaw open. "She's here, with us?"

"Yes," said Pammy, smiling. "And she's a charming girl who only wants to be helpful."

"Well," said Julia sarcastically. "She sure has a funny way of showing it by locking the filing cabinets in the middle of the day and emptying drawers of supplies."

"You are right there. And that's not all she's done," said Pammy. "But, if you think about it, in the beginning, we just heard noises, but I immediately gave her a very mean name. And, we started blaming her for everything, even when the printer broke down."

No one spoke. Pammy continued. "I feel bad for doing that. You know, if you're going to be blamed for things, you might as well do what you're being blamed for, right?"

Silence. Crickets. They all looked at each other, nodding. It was decided right there and then that changes would immediately be implemented. Scary Mary became Lovely Louisa. Instead of acting like a nuisance, Louisa started helping around the office. Staplers never ran out of staples. Printers and copiers never needed to be refilled with paper, ink, or toner. Charts seemed just to show up wherever required, and best of all, Julia didn't need to order any more supplies. Lovely Louisa took on that task.

From that day forward, they learned that even ghosts needed appreciation.

A PUZZLING MYSTERY

A PUZZLING MYSTERY

Mable Miller did as she always would and perched herself at the square table situated in the living room of the Open Arms retirement home. Open Arms wasn't your typical home for older folks. Living in this beautiful establishment was more privileged than one would think. It was privately owned and operated and thus exclusive to some degree.

Acres of beautiful grounds, a gourmet chef, and rooms more like sophisticated suites than standard rooms, made this residence very sought after. The outside was a Tudor made of brick with large half-timbered white stucco siding sections, giving it a medieval appearance. It was easily the most delightful structure for miles. When Mable spoke of it to her friends still in their private homes, she refused to talk of its cost. She had, instead, a favorite phrase.

"It costs a pretty penny, you know," she would say with upstretched eyebrows emphasizing the point. No one knew what to say to this, so they often did not respond. Mable much preferred it that way. Mable considered herself a plain lady. However, her maturity, confidence, and independence were only superseded by the twinkle in her eyes and peachy skin.

This cozy autumn afternoon, Mable sat at that exact spot as she did on most days, in front of several puzzle pieces covering the table. Having separated the puzzle parts into categories, she constructed the outer edge. One thousand pieces was not exactly a challenge for her. However, the autumn landscaped picture would prove to be just that with all its earth tones.

Having separated the shades into piles, she slowly fit them into place, seemingly stumped, judging by the deep breaths exhaled. With no hurry necessary, Mable stayed put and carefully studied the layout in front of her. That's when she was joined by a familiar, if not sometimes annoying, puzzle partner who dropped down in the chair adjacent.

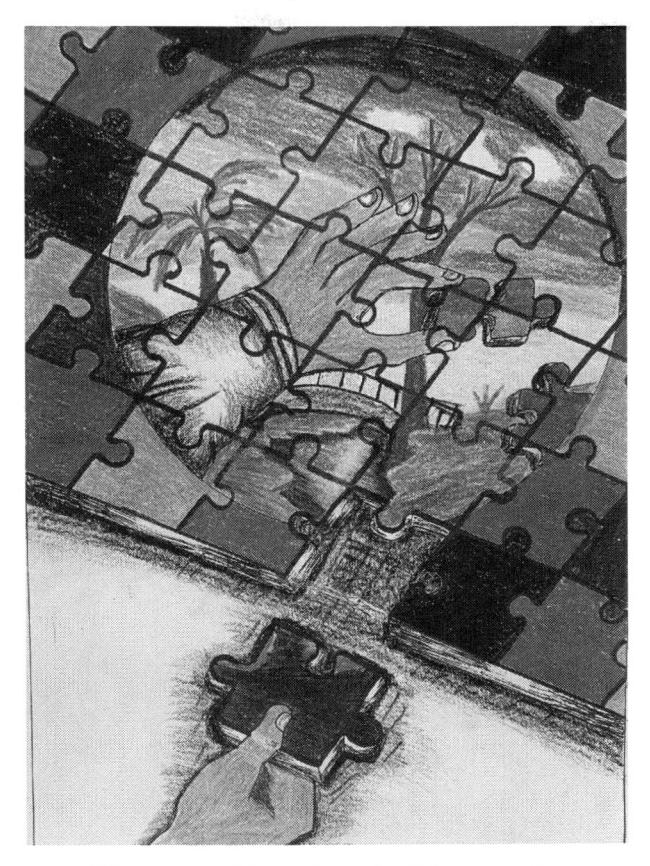

Illustrated by: Maria Hernandez

Archie Jones was one year older than Mable, but no one discussed age at Open Arms. As most residents called him, Archie was what many called a man of few words. Fairly tall with what Mable would call a distinguished chin and graying hair, he was well known as being one of the nicest and quietest guys at Open Arms. Maybe that's why he and Mable got along so well. Mable and Archie could sit beside one another for hours, working on a puzzle without saying a word. Many visitors mistook them for a married couple.

Mable wore a delicate pink dress covered in tiny white polka dots, all the way mid-calf length. She was enormously proud of the fact that she often wore light pink nail polish. Most female residents didn't bother with such frivolities anymore. More than this, Mable wore shoes to match her ensembles and always had her hair impeccably styled. She swore by Beatrice, her favorite stylist at the nearby Silver Bells Hair Salon. Archie wouldn't consider her plain.

Archie contrasted greatly with his brown pants and matching brown plaid button-up shirt, like most everything else in his wardrobe in his suite. His sandy waved hair, tamed only by a few brush strokes, completed his easygoing look. He was a simple man, and that's why Mable thought so much of him. Mable came to Open Arms after Archie, and they became friends almost instantly.

Archie glanced around the table at the piles of puzzle pieces, slowly picked up one seemingly arbitrary piece, and snapped it into place with what looked like ease. Mable rarely let on, but Archie relished that she found his gift frustrating. This time, she couldn't help but voice it. And he enjoyed it immensely.

"That is so annoying," she said without looking in his direction. Without needing to, she knew he was slightly grinning.

Adding insult to injury, he picked up another and placed it inside the frame on Mable's side. Mable, realizing that its place was only half an inch from where it lay, sighed in disgust, knowing he was patronizing her. Before she could let out another sigh, a much older and thoroughly cantankerous woman by the name of Sylvia put in the last of her three-thousand-piece puzzle and clapped victoriously for herself.

"What an arrogant woman," said Mable under her breath while wrinkling her nose in disgust. "Such a showoff."

"Now, Mable," Archie said placatingly. "She does much larger puzzles in half the time we do." Mable shot a piercing look out the corners of her eyes back at him. He knew it best to consider the conversation closed.

Sylvia Wilkshire, with her curly permed hair, high-class

clothes, and immense sense of self-worth, looked at others as if she was looking down upon ants on the ground. And every resident was well aware of this fact. The nurses always tried to smooth things over.

"That's beautiful," said Nurse Jenkins, stopping to look while balancing a tray on the palms of her hands. "You did an excellent job."

Sylvia beamed in pride, her hands in a clasp in front of her chest, looking like a peacock. Another worker stopped to look at her finished puzzle and smiled widely also.

Mable took a deep breath and sighed loud enough for everyone to hear. Archie looked at her as if questioning her about her thoughts, but before he could ask, she suddenly rose and spoke abruptly.

"I'm going to bed," Mable said with a tone Archie knew better than to question. It would be stupid to cross Mable, and Archie wasn't a stupid man.

"I'll walk you to your room," Archie answered as he took her by the arm and began to move from the living room area.

They slowly climbed one flight of stairs, and as they approached the door to Mable's room, he turned to face her. She could tell by the look on his face that he disapproved of her attitude, but she continued her case before he could speak.

"Now, Archie," she pleaded. "You know as well as I do that she's a thoroughly unpleasant woman."

He started to mumble in response, and without listening, she muttered above his. When they both stopped simultaneously, they stared at each other and began to smile. He raised his arms and grabbed her forearms gently. She took a deep breath.

"I understand how you feel," he said warmly. "But she's just the way she is, and she's never going to change."

She smiled back at him. "So, I guess we are just stuck with her until she's gone." They both shot broad smiles at one another.

"Good night, Mable," said Archie softly.

"Good night," Mable returned as she disappeared behind her door.

Archie shook his head, chuckling at Mable's orneriness, and began to ascend the stairs to the third floor and his suite. He stopped short at hearing what sounded like the floorboards squeaking below him. Mable's puzzle partner bent down to see if anyone was under the stairs but only saw darkness. Tired, he continued to his room and went to bed.

***

THE FOLLOWING DAY brought flashing lights, men trekking back and forth on the property in uniforms and badges, and many sad faces quietly thinking about how much they disliked the victim, rolled out on a gurney. Nurses consoled residents with pats on their shoulders and cups of coffee. A somber mood fell heavy on all of them.

Archie found his friend in the back corner of the sitting room off the living room. She looked down at the floor and then rose to gaze at the backyard, which appeared to console her. Archie strolled toward her, then lowered onto a love seat once Mable did the same. She must have been in another world as she didn't seem to notice him.

"Mable," he asked. "Why are you sitting here all by yourself?"

His sweet friend slowly turned to face him with tears filling her eyes. Saddened, he pinched his mouth and nodded validation. Without a word, she knew that he fully understood her feelings. Her eyes closed, and she sighed while collapsing into his arms. Mable and Archie rarely hugged, but indeed, this was an exception.

Mable, deciding this had gone on long enough, inhaled deeply and sat up. While wiping her eyes, Archie directed the conversation.

"Mable," he said quietly. "You were right. She was a thoroughly unpleasant woman, just like you said."

Mable gasped. "Oh, please don't remind me of what I said. I was so cruel."

"You aren't the only one who felt that way about her."

"Maybe not," she nearly snorted. "But, I'm the only one who said it out loud." Mable grabbed her mouth in a desperate attempt to keep from crying harder. Her tender heart was only one thing he admired about her.

"Oh," he said, leaning down to look her square in the eyes. "Don't be foolish." He looked behind him to assure privacy and then back at her. "That's absolutely untrue. Just now, I overheard Nurses Lewis and Hamstein saying how sad it was but also how the mood of this home will improve now that she's gone."

"No, they didn't," she rebuked. She felt he might have been just saying this to make her feel better.

"Yes, they said it. I heard it. And they are two of the nicest people I know."

"They are very nice usually," she said, furrowing her brows.

"Not just usually," he corrected. "They are lovely people, but they are human. No one can fault them for feeling the way they do."

"I guess not," said Mable wiping tears from her face. "Sylvia treated them shamefully on more than one occasion."

"Exactly," he agreed soothingly. His brown eyes, ironically matching everything he wore, softened. "So stop being so hard on yourself."

She looked back out the window and smiled at the tree limbs gently lifting under the breeze. Her lips formed a half smile while looking back at her friend, and she nodded. They rose, and he took her arm to walk her to join the others. He led her over to an empty area so no one would hear. Before entering the other room, he leaned in and whispered.

"And I heard Erma telling Tilly that now they might be able to get some hot water for bathing." Mable frowned in disgust. "Oh come now, you know as well as I do that Sylvia loved stealing all the hot water."

She laughed out loud. Through the threshold, they rejoined the other residents. Nurses passed out hot coffee to help soothe the unrest in the room. At the same time, they sipped the steamy beverage, the room filled with soothing conversation. Somehow, the night seemed a little less sad by bedtime.

Later that same evening, Mable exited her suite in a nightgown, robe, and slippers on her way down to the study to exchange books. Hoping to find a mystery with a steamy male protagonist, she danced her eyes over book covers on the shelves. Her search was interrupted by mumbled voices coming from the back hallway and Sylvia's rooms. She paused her search and listened with wide eyes.

Mable hurriedly grabbed a book and quietly tiptoed in that direction, but not leaving the study. She listened from inside the threshold area and hoped they would mumble just a little more loudly. Then, she heard two nurses walk out of Sylvia's room and decided it best to sprint back to the bookshelves to feign a continued search in case they saw her. Without noticing Mable, they walked past the doorway and into a back room off the foyer, presumably carrying boxes containing Sylvia's belongings. Boxes of puzzles sticking out, one slipped and slammed to the floor. Mable resisted the urge to gasp and startle too loudly by covering her mouth with her fingertips. Nurse Hamstein leaned down to retrieve it, and Mable's eyes widened even more. Mable was sure it was not a possession of the late resident. In fact, she had never seen that puzzle box anywhere in the home before now.

She remained still and quiet, not wishing to be seen, deciding it better to let this slide. She didn't want anyone to think she was snooping, even though she actually was. After the nurses disappeared around the corner, Mable grabbed the chosen book again and tried to slither up the stairs. She stopped in surprise when she heard the nurses talking from the other side of the wall.

"As nasty as Mrs. Wilkshire was, I wouldn't be surprised if someone helped her along," said one nurse to the other. "I'm sure many have at least thought about it."

Mable felt as if she couldn't get up the stairs fast enough. She sighed in relief as she shut her door tight. Her bed was comfy enough, but sleep didn't come too quickly this night.

***

THE FOLLOWING DAY brought sunshine beams through the breakfast room windows. Archie and Mable sat quietly at a small corner table, sipping coffee and munching scrambled eggs. Mable never cared for the scrambled eggs at Open Arms as she liked them made with heavy whipping cream. Her granddaughter called them Fancy Eggs.

Archie noticed she was picking at her eggs and smiled, knowing why. He didn't bring it up because he knew better than that. He was just about to compliment her on her new outfit when the front doorbell rang. He noticed a slight jump and a startle from his breakfast companion.

"Good morning, ma'am," said a stern, authoritative male voice from the direction of the foyer.

"Good morning," answered Nurse Jenkins. "How can I help you?"

"My credentials, ma'am," he then stated, followed by a snapping noise presumably made by him shutting his wallet.

Mable ignored what was left of her breakfast in front of her and turned her head backward to best hear. Archie, seeing no reason to waste a good breakfast, ate on.

"I'm Chief Inspector Saunders, and this is Sergeant Davis," he retorted.

"Oh," answered Nurse Jenkins with a rise in her voice. This indicated to Mable that they were in plain clothes; otherwise, Nurse Jenkins would not be surprised. Nothing much got past Mable.

"Is the owner on the premises?" he asked. The nurse must have welcomed them in and shut the door.

"No. The owners live out of state, but Nurse Lewis is our manager," she answered. "She's in the back working on schedules."

"Is there somewhere private back there where we can talk with her?" a different male voice asked, more than likely the sergeant.

"Oh yes," answered Nurse Jenkins. "I can take you to her office if you will just follow me this way."

Footsteps dropped upon the foyer and then into the hall, which led through the dining area. The three traveled through the far end of the room and then into a second hallway leading to the back. Mable and Archie traded a glance with the officers, who were both wearing beige-colored overcoats. After they disappeared, Archie looked back at his breakfast plate, and Mable turned back around only to stare straight out of the window.

***

BACK IN NURSE LEWIS'S PRIVATE OFFICE, the two detectives were shown in and took seats in front of her large, ornate desk. Sergeant Davis pulled out a small notebook while Chief Inspector Saunders introduced them both once again and began to explain the reason for their visit. All three took a seat.

"Hello, ma'am," said the chief inspector. "You're probably wondering why we're here."

The manager raised her eyebrows slightly and answered without hesitation. "My name is Debbie Lewis, and you are right. I am wondering why you're here; it can't be good news surely."

The chief inspector looked at his sergeant and then again to the mid-thirties and slightly attractive retirement home manager. He hardly needed his trained observation skills to see her piercing blue eyes, trim physique, and warm smile. Momentarily, he forgot what he was going to say.

Snapping out of the trance, he continued. "Sergeant Davis and I are here about the sudden death of one of your residents. Sylvia Wilkshire."

The manager shook her head and looked down toward folded hands sitting upon her desk. "It's so very sad. One day, she was happily putting together puzzles, and then by the next morning, she was gone."

"Did Mrs. Wilkshire have any health problems?" asked the sergeant, clearly able to see that his superior was somewhat distracted.

"Well, yes," answered Nurse Lewis. "But all our residents here have some sort of health issue, if not several."

"Can you tell us what was wrong with this resident, in particular?"

"Well, she took medicine for high blood pressure, and she had a minor skin issue, so she used a topical medication. There were a lot of heart issues in her family, and with her having high blood pressure, we figured that she would eventually develop something with her heart too." The nurse manager sighed. "We certainly didn't think that she would have a heart attack so soon."

"Nurse Lewis, we wouldn't be here if it were a simple heart attack," the chief inspector said as gently as he knew.

Simultaneously, she gasped while he spoke, realizing suddenly why they were in her office. "Oh, no," she said, lowering the volume of her voice. "Don't tell me."

Sergeant Davis jumped in. "I'm afraid it doesn't look like natural causes."

"I don't understand. The ambulance workers said Sylvia was a victim of a heart attack."

Neither of the officers in suits spoke at that time. They remained silent to give her a little more time to adjust to the news.

"She did have a heart attack, right?" she asked.

The chief inspector decided to step up and chimed in authoritatively this time. "Our doctors tell us she did have a heart attack but not from natural causes. Can you tell my sergeant what Mrs. Wilkshire had to eat and drink yesterday?"

As the manager stammered and stuttered to remember the meals served, Saunders took a scan around the office. He wasn't sure what he thought he would find, but he did happen upon some boxes containing a resident's possessions, sitting off in the corner.

Chief Inspector Saunders was a muscular man of about forty-eight years of age, with dark eyes and hair and a very tidy appearance. His suit fit him perfectly, and he was immaculately clean. However, discreet patience wasn't a strong suit for him.

"What's that?" he asked while pointing in the direction of the corner of her office and the boxes. Realizing that he interrupted, his face blushed slightly, and he added, "My apologies for interrupting."

The manager smiled a bit more widely while rising to walk over to the boxes in question. She bent down and picked up an article from one of them. "These are a few of Sylvia's things. We just started to pack things up last night."

"Already?" asked the chief inspector. "Excuse me for saying so but isn't that a little soon?"

Nurse Lewis looked up at him out of the top of her eyes with a disappointed aim affixed. She didn't need to speak a word to communicate her annoyance with his question.

"I mean, it's only been one day since her death," he backpedaled. "Do you always start packing up residents' belongings this quickly after they pass?"

She sighed and nodded. "Not usually, but her daughter called us yesterday afternoon and asked us how soon we could gather her things. She's only in town for a few days and wants to take them with her when she leaves. She's hoping to take her mother's body to the crematorium as soon as possible so she can transport her back to her home for burial." She moved a few items around in one of the boxes to better arrange. "She lives in Ticking County, which is about one hour away. She didn't get here often due to having a very demanding job back there."

"Kind of a coincidence her being here right when her mother dies, wouldn't you say?" said the chief inspector. His sergeant nodded in agreement.

"I see what you mean," agreed Nurse Lewis.

"Well, those boxes will have to be immediately returned to her room and, except for my men, will be off-limits to anyone."

"Anyone?" she asked without waiting to get an answer. She realized he wasn't backing down. "Alright, I'll have them taken right back."

"No," the chief inspector barked and then quieted his tone. "I'm sorry. Sergeant Davis will return them. No one but my men should go into Sylvia's suite at all from this moment onward."

"I see," said the nurse, accepting his orders with grace.

"Nurse Lewis, I have to tell you that a poisonous substance was found in Mrs. Wilkshire's body."

"What? No way." Nurse Lewis became unexpectedly louder than she had realized.

"Please lower your voice," said the chief inspector. "I'm afraid so. We are not at liberty to disclose the name of the substance, but until my men have a chance to inspect your kitchen and pantries, the food for the residents will have to be obtained elsewhere."

"What an inconvenience," said the nurse manager. "But, I see why. Just for the record, we don't poison our residents, chief inspector."

He smiled. "I'm sure you don't." He tried to smooth over the troubled waters. "I'm sure it will be established that the poison did not come from your kitchen. Just to follow protocol, Sergeant Davis will be putting a police lock on her suite and the kitchen doors."

"If you must," she acquiesced.

"I'm afraid we must," said the sergeant, trying to shoot her a look of understanding. When he left, he was betting money that Nurse Lewis's feathers were anything but smooth.

***

Archie and Mable sat in the dining room in front of a chicken breast and potatoes supper. The police search of the Open Arms kitchen resulted in no poisons or suspicious substances, so the kitchen was now officially reopened. Archie tried to make small talk. Mable looked distracted, staring straight through anything in front of her eyes,

"Mable," Archie asked. "Are you alright?"

Mable didn't respond. Archie sighed in frustration. He picked up his drink and slurped loudly, knowing that annoying her was a sure-fire way to get her attention. Mable broke out of her trance and glared at her companion.

"I asked you if you were alright," he asserted quickly before being the recipient of her wrath. Archie set his drink back down on the table. "You have been miles away. I have been trying to talk to you."

"I'm sorry," she admitted.

"What is it, Mable?" he pleaded.

"It's just something I can't get out of my head," she said, looking down at her plate. "It might not mean anything at all."

Mable lowered the volume of her voice as two residents

walked past, smiling at her. She smiled back at them as they left the dining area. After seeing them go, she turned back to Archie and continued to explain in a whisper.

"It was the puzzle," she said with emphasis as if Archie would understand. He didn't.

"The puzzle?" he asked, only to be told to talk more softly with a "quiet" from Mable. "I don't understand," he said in a whisper as instructed.

"That night," she went on. "The night after Sylvia died, I came downstairs at night after everyone had gone to bed to exchange books in the library."

"OK," he said. "What about it?"

"Let me finish." She pushed her plate forward and leaned on the table with her forearms. "While I was down here, I heard the nurses in Sylvia's room. They must have been boxing up her belongings. Anyways, I stayed behind the wall in the library and heard them come out carrying boxes. One box was stacked full of puzzle boxes."

"That makes sense," agreed Archie. "We all know that Sylvia had a lot of puzzles."

"Yes, she did, but one fell out of the box. I saw it lying on the floor before they picked it up." She paused. Archie became annoyed.

"And?" he asked impatiently.

"And," she said, leaning in towards him whispering even more. He leaned in to match her. "It wasn't her puzzle."

Illustrated by: Ryleigh Hornbeck

Mable nodded her head as if she had solved one of the great

mysteries of the world and sipped from her coffee cup.

Archie, more confused than ever, sighed deeply. He also took a sip of coffee, letting what she had just shared sink in a little. Unfortunately, it made no sense to him, and he sat staring at her silently.

"Don't you see?" she explained. "Sylvia never kept someone else's puzzle box in her room. If she borrowed one, it would sit on a table out here until she finished it, and then she would give it right back to the owner. You know how particular she was. And she would never steal something. I think you would have to agree with me there." Her eyebrows raised toward her hairline.

"You know, you're right about that." He paused and then continued. "I have no idea what it means, but you do have a point. There is absolutely no reason Sylvia should have a puzzle that wasn't hers in her room." He took another sip from his cup. "Hmmm."

"Hmmm is right," said Mable with conviction. After several sips of coffee, she overheard Nurse Lewis talking with the police officers investigating the death as they walked in the back garden. Mable and Archie's table was by the garden window, so listening was a reasonably easy task. Mable shot an ornery glance at Archie, and the two of them rose from the table and sat in the bay window area, in perfect view of the garden, and the three in conversation.

Archie leaned in. "We shouldn't be eavesdropping."

"I dare say we shouldn't, but that's what we are doing," she said. "Ssshhh."

Despite muffled voices through closed windows, the conversation was still easily understood. Mable and Archie heard the chief inspector ask more questions about Sylvia's daughter. More than that, he told her that when the police talked to her, she never mentioned the fact that she was only in town for a few days. And she also didn't tell them she was in a hurry for her mother's body to be released either.

Mable made a split-second decision when she saw the inspector heading for his car. She bolted out of the retirement home with Archie on her heels. She caught the inspector right before he stepped into his car.

"Inspector," she called. "Inspector, I need to talk to you. It's vital."

The inspector stopped and turned. "I'm in a hurry, madam."

"I have information pertaining to the death of Sylvia Wilkshire."

***

THE LOCAL POLICE STATION sat in the middle of town between Maggie's Fashions and a quaint café. The courthouse sat across the street from all three of them. Three small rooms located in the back of the police station allocated for the inspectors buzzed with a feeling of unrest. Mable and Archie sat at a conference table, providing their vital information. Chief Inspector Saunders stood looking out a small window while Sergeant Davis took notes.

"Let me get this right," repeated Davis. "You say that Sylvia's belongings included a puzzle box that didn't belong to her. Do you suppose she stole it?"

"Absolutely not," insisted Mable with furrowed brows and flared nostrils. She looked at Archie, who laughed out of astonishment.

"Now look here," said Archie. "Sylvia was not what one would call a nice person, but she definitely did not steal…ever."

The chief inspector turned around abruptly. Frustrated, his associate seemed surprised that his superior didn't put a stop to the meeting. Instead, he asked a set of unexpected questions.

"Ma'am, what makes you think Mrs. Wilkshire wouldn't have stolen the puzzle?"

Mable sighed a breath, spread her lips into a smile, and answered with a confident tone. "Because, Inspector, although she was arrogant and bragged constantly, she never lied, and she never stole. When you lived together as closely as we all do at Open Arms, you really get to know people."

The sergeant looked at Archie, who added a proud smile and nodded in agreement. Both colleagues looked at each other and thanked them for the information and for coming in. As Archie took Mable's arm, he walked her out of the station and began the short walk back to their retirement home. Saunders smiled as he watched them walk away through a window while Davis shut his notebook in disappointment. The chief inspector couldn't help but enjoy the sweet, old couple.

THE NEXT DAY, Open Arms retirement home felt anything but usual. Sergeant Davis and two uniformed officers arrived early to rifle through Sylvia's room. Unfortunately, the residents greeted them with several simmered glares followed by disgruntled mumbles. The residents saw them as intrusive and didn't like the idea of a dead person's life and belongings spread out in the open for all to see. Sylvia's death, formally announced as a murder, didn't seem to change their opinion of that. Not releasing the name of the poison was essential to the investigation but left residents with a feeling of disbelief and distrust.

Crime scene tape covered the entrance to Sylvia's bedroom, but that didn't stop residents from standing on the outside of that tape, gawking in as they searched. This would be out of character for Mable, but the fact that everyone was doing it at one time or another allowed her the opportunity to use the excuse of bad manners to take a peek. Archie knew all too well what she was doing and sat with his arms crossed over his chest, grinning at his cunning lady friend.

One of the officers looked up and presented her with a placating smile matching the others before and spoke to Mable in a childlike tone.

"Ma'am, I'm sorry, but I'm going to have to ask you to step away from this area," he said.

Mable bought time as she used every second to take in everything each of the three was doing. "I'm sorry, young man," she responded in an equally placating manner. "Nurse Lewis said the tape was to keep everyone out of this room. She didn't say we weren't allowed to stand on the outside of it."

In a matter of seconds, her eyes scanned the layout of the room and the fact that her dresser, wardrobe, and closets were turned out and searched already. The boxes of puzzles in the corner looked undisturbed and much the same as they were when she secretly saw the nurse taking them out.

"I'm sure that's true, but we still need you to leave," answered the young officer.

At that moment, Sergeant Davis looked up from his search, turned around, and looked straight at Mable. He sighed and forcefully released his breath from puffy cheeks in exasperation.

He dropped an item from a drawer and stomped his way over drawers, umbrellas, and much everything else strewn over the floor.

Before he could attack, Mable put him on the defensive. "Sergeant Davis," she scolded. "You should be ashamed of yourself, making such a mess of Sylvia's room."

He motioned for his assisting officer to return to his search, leaned down, and lowered his voice. "Mable, I appreciated you coming down to the station and telling us what you know, but you must leave us alone to complete this search."

"Oh, I'm sure you must, Sergeant Davis," she said, lowering her eyes, hoping this would cause him to be more lenient on her. "But, look at the mess."

Mable made a mental note of the room, hoping to see something that might be important. However, the sergeant did not move from his spot, peering at her. Once done, she returned her gaze to him, flashed her eyes, and smiled again as if they were best of friends.

"Isn't there some activity you could attend? Bingo? Cards?"

Mable found this disrespectful and was just about to pounce

on him when Archie showed up just in time to whisk her away. He interrupted whatever it was she was about to say back to him as he gently curled her arm around his.

"Now come, Mable," he said lovingly. "Let's let these men get on with their important work, shall we?" He patted her hand, which rested on his forearm, and they both turned around. When out of sight of the officers, Mable shot a very ornery grin at Archie.

Walking away, he whispered, "See anything?"

She lifted her free hand and pointed to her platinum-dyed head of hair. "You know me. I've got it all stored right up here." He raised his eyebrows at her while grinning. They returned to the sitting room and sat in a love seat in a quiet and private corner.

"Now," said Archie in a hushed voice. "Let's have it."

"You know there are three of them. One is emptying her cedar chest, another is taking her clothes out of closets, and the sergeant is going through her dresser drawers." She paused to make sure no one was listening. "They seem to be making quite a thorough search."

"Of that, I have no doubt," answered Archie.

Mable went on to list everything she saw in detail all around the rooms of Sylvia Wilkshire to Archie's amazement. Tiny pieces of information did not escape her cunning eye or remarkable memory.

"You are truly amazing. I don't know how you can remember everything as if you are looking right at it." Mable furrowed her brows and sighed. Archie waited for her to continue, but she did not.

"Mable," he said, putting his hand on her shoulder. "What is it?"

Mable played nervously with the ruffles on the sleeve of her chiffon floral top. "I'm not sure, but I think something wasn't right in her room."

Archie turned his face in the general direction of the room in question. "Well, with everything thrown all over the place, surely—" Mable interrupted.

"No, it had nothing to do with any of that," she insisted. "I just can't think exactly what it was, but something wasn't right." She sighed. "Why is my photographic memory failing me now of all times?"

"OK," said Archie. "Let's go through some ideas. Something was there that shouldn't be there?"

"No," answered Mable without hesitation.

"Something missing?"

"I don't think it was that either," she said with her face slightly scrunched in deep thought.

"Well, seeing that it was a mess with their search—" Archie added. Once again, Mable interrupted.

"I know it's hard to believe that I could notice something awry considering all the mess, but I know something was odd. I just know it."

Archie pulled her closer into his chest with his arm firmly across her shoulders. With a peck on her forehead, Mable didn't doubt his trust. But he wanted to make sure she knew.

"I don't doubt you for one second, Mable," he proclaimed. And they let themselves fall onto the back of the love seat, resting. Fifteen minutes later, he convinced her to let it all go for a while and work with him on a new puzzle.

***

Back at the station, Sergeant Davis reported to his superior, who laid back in his office chair with his feet crossed upon his desk. Davis stood and paced at times, reading from a small notebook that lay open in his hand. The latter seemed intent on studying the ceiling.

"So, here's what we know," said Sergeant Davis. "Mrs. Wilkshire is rich, which would provide a motive for her daughter."

"Yeah, the daughter who left out certain things about herself when we questioned her and who is in a hurry to get her mother cremated and buried."

"Yeah," continued Davis. "The search of her room also uncovered some, shall we say, bizarre bits of information."

"Like what?" asked his superior.

"She was spying on people, sir." The sergeant emphasized this sentence.

"So what?" the latter replied. "Old biddies are always spying on each other. They know when someone takes too many sugar cubes in their coffee or when another stole a cookie from the snack cart. It's called they have nothing better to do."

The two officers shared a laugh. Saunders sniffed and removed his feet from his desk. He rose to warm his cup of coffee with the small pot they kept in their office. Davis sipped from his bottle of water.

"All kidding aside, sir," said Davis. "It's a bit more serious than that. And she has it all written down in a little notebook we found at the bottom of her cedar chest."

"What?" asked Saunders, still unconvinced. "Let me guess. Fred is sneaking kisses with Ethel under the staircase, right?"

"No, it's more like she witnessed a nurse taking drinks of alcohol when on duty by herself at night."

Saunders perked up. "Really?"

"Yeah, and it gets worse." Davis opened the notebook in question, handed it over to Saunders, and pointed out specific entries. "Look at who is forging the medication records and taking pain meds for herself."

"That's insane," Saunders belted out. "The patient can tell."

"Not if they're a dementia patient. I'm sure they forget taking meds, eating meals, and getting dressed every day."

"Get on the horn, Davis," instructed Saunders. "Tell Nurse Lewis we're going to need to know the diagnosis of each and every resident."

Davis picked up the phone. "I'm sure she's not going to allow that."

Saunders picked up the phone on his desk too and answered his sergeant. "I'll be getting a search warrant from Judge Limbacher to make sure she has no other choice."

***

"Well, that was easy," said Davis, holding up a fax from Open Arms retirement home and Nurse Lewis.

"I think the fact that the judge weighed in had something to do with it," Saunders smiled.

Saunders assigned Davis to match up names and diagnoses with Sylvia Wilkshire's notebook entries. Sylvia wasn't clear in naming names, so this would be tougher than it looked at first. Sylvia was definitely no dummy. Davis spent hours working on this and had very little to show for it. His eyes grew heavy while his suit tie began to hang loose and lower. Coffee no longer doing the trick this dark evening, Davis allowed his eyes to close.

Meanwhile, Saunders sat in his lonely apartment reading and rereading the medical examiner's report. Rubbing his eyes, he turned to Mrs. Wilkshire's financial records. *Phew! Three million dollars would be a tidy sum worth killing for. The daughter seems nice enough, but I can't rule her out.* Yawning, taking over, Saunders' mind decided to quit for the night.

Meanwhile, back at Open Arms, the only sound coming from the common area downstairs was the *tick-tock* of the grandfather clock standing in the foyer. The darkened house settled; however, there wasn't a soul there to hear it. Not even the nurse on duty heard. She was otherwise engaged in the heavy breathing sounds of sleep rising up and down from inside the office. Just then, a ruffling on the staircase joined the silence.

Archie insisted that if Mable followed through with her plan of putting sleeping medication in Nurse Hamstein's nighttime cocoa, he would be there with her. He made it clear that he disapproved of her strategy, but regardless, he couldn't sleep if she took this chance alone. Archie considered himself Mable's protector, especially when the plan was as risky as this.

Archie's little granddaughter taught him to put his cell phone on silent vibrate, so he set both his and Mable's the same before they snuck downstairs. Archie stood on guard around the corner from Nurse Hamstein to ensure she didn't wake while hiding himself behind a large plant.

Mable removed the crime scene tape and started her investigation in Sylvia's room. After she remembered what wasn't right in this suite, this plan came about. Mable was startled and insisted that Archie take her for a short walk in the garden earlier in the evening. When alone, she exclaimed that Sylvia's floor rug was out of place. That was what wasn't right in Sylvia's room.

Archie insisted that the officers must have moved it during the search, but Mable reminded him that Sylvia always secured her floor rugs with tape. He couldn't argue with this point and agreed to help her test the theory. As he watched the sleeping nurse, he vacillated between feelings of guilt and hope: guilt about spiking her cocoa, and hope that they put in enough to keep her asleep long enough.

Mable struck gold and soon was on the threshold, signaling Archie to join her. She held a thick and professional-looking notebook in her arms but refused to talk until upstairs. They replaced the crime scene tape and hurried back upstairs.

After looking through it, they both agreed it was too risky for Mable to keep it in her room, and he put it in the safe in his room, brought from his stately mansion. He walked Mable back to her door and hugged her. At that moment, a neighbor's door opened just a sliver, and they knew they were being spied upon. Mable shrugged her shoulders, closed the door, and went to sleep. Archie sauntered past the neighbor's door, grinning at assumptions and gossip that would swirl tomorrow at breakfast.

***

BREAKFAST WAS AS STRANGE as Archie had predicted. Mumbles, residents were looking at the two of them, nudging each other and laughing under their breath. The big news making its way around the rumor mill was a lovers' rendezvous. Archie and Mable allowed them to think as they liked. They decided it was better than letting them know they were investigating.

"I still can't believe where you found that fancy notebook," said Archie in between bites.

"Well, I knew something was wrong in Sylvia's room that day the police were searching," she answered.

"But for you to notice the moved rug, well, that was brilliant," he said with a smile. "Who would have thought that Sylvia would take the time to pry up floorboards to make a hiding place for the notebook?"

"If she didn't need to cover scratches with the rug, I would never have found it," admitted Mable. She then noticed Archie was refilling his breakfast plate with second helpings. "Archie, do you think you could finish up? I'm afraid we'll be late for our appointment with the chief inspector." Mable managed to lower her volume to a whisper.

Archie shoved the last of a muffin into his mouth and gulped his coffee, nearly choking. Mable gently patted his back while simultaneously pulling him through the dining room and out the front door. Mable sported a rather large bag containing, among other things, Sylvia's secret notebook.

Running out the front door of Open Arms, a female resident

called out to Mable. "Where's the fire?"

Mable didn't look back. However, Archie turned and answered, smiling back. "That new mystery film's out down at the cinema. Catching the matinee."

When the two approached the local cinema, they took a sharp left and puttered down the street to a familiar city building. Inside, they were lucky to find the two officers they needed. They decided to get straight to the point, not knowing how long their patience would last.

"Chief Inspector, thank you for seeing us at such short notice," Mable said while taking a seat.

The sergeant pulled up another chair for Archie, who sat to her right. One officer held the dark and thick notebook while the other looked, leaning over, each one looking up at the retired couple from time to time. Mable did most of the talking, and Archie sat proudly listening.

"It was under the floorboards, you see. That's why you never found it, Sergeant," Mable calmly explained.

Chief Inspector Saunders shot piercing eyes toward his sergeant. The latter cleared his throat in embarrassment.

"Now, Chief Inspector, don't fault the boy. He wasn't to know where the rug should have been," placated Mable. Again, Archie sat with his arms folded across his chest, grinning.

"The rug, ma'am?" asked Sergeant Davis.

"Yes, the rug, young man," she answered. "You see, Sylvia always kept that rug by the washstand, but the day you came to search, it was moved over by the bed."

"And the significance of the rug?" asked the older of the two officers.

"It hid the secret hiding place, of course," Mable said with apparent certainty.

The sergeant moved restlessly under the scrutiny of his boss. "I see," said the superior.

"Now, there was no way for your young officer to know. Sylvia always secured her rugs with carpet tape."

"So," said the boss. "Moving on to this notebook," he said as he scrolled through the pages slowly.

"I think that's where I come in, Chief Inspector," said Archie. "I'm not entirely sure, but to me, it looks like a log of some sort."

"Yes, I see what you mean," said the chief inspector. "If I didn't know any better, I would say your Mrs. Wilkshire had a nose for nosing around."

"Yes, that's one way to put it," laughed Archie. He quickly dimmed his smile, realizing the seriousness of the situation. "I used to be a security guard, and this notebook looks a lot like how we used to log during our shift. Who did what. Who left when. What we heard, et cetera."

The chief inspector handed the notebook over to his partner. "A lot of people wouldn't be happy with her recording their secrets," the sergeant said. "She might have happened upon a secret that got her killed."

As they got up to leave, the officers thanked them and reprimanded them for snooping. Archie and Mable promised this would be the very last time. The officers agreed to carefully look through the notebook and insisted that the two amateur sleuths not tell anyone about their find.

MYSTERIOUS TALES OF THE UNEXPLAINED: VOLUME II

Illustrated by: Rilee Pershing

"Fair enough," said Mable, grabbing her purse. As she walked away, she stopped short and turned on her heels. "Oh, I almost forgot to mention another strange thing I noticed. There was a puzzle box on the top of those boxes that sat in the corner of her room."

"There were a lot of puzzles, ma'am," said the sergeant. "You know as well as I that Mrs. Wilkshire loved puzzles."

"Yes, young man," Mable said as she shook her head and snapped her tongue over her teeth. "But, this wasn't one of her puzzles. It didn't belong. Anyways, the strange thing is that it's gone."

"Gone?" asked the chief inspector.

"Yes, when I was in there the other night, I thought I heard someone coming, and so I hopped into the corner by the boxes. When I looked down with my little flashlight, I noticed right away that it was gone. It was such a pretty puzzle with the picture of a snowy scene, with a deer and a pond. It was all shimmery. I never saw one with sparkles like that." There was a pause. "I don't know what it could mean, but I wanted to remember to tell you."

Mable grabbed Archie's arm and directed him toward the door. "You know," she said with a sparkle in her eyes, "if we hurry, we can just make that film at the cinema."

"Oh yes," Archie agreed, looking at his wristwatch. "And I have a two-for-one coupon for buttered popcorn."

"Oh, that's great," she said back as they walked as fast as they could for the door.

Later that same day, as the officers combed through the notebook found in Sylvia Wilkshire's secret hiding place, they gasped at the enormity of her log and found more than one motive for murder. But how could they prove who did it? Sergeant Davis smacked his hand on the top of his desk.

"The puzzle," he forcefully said. "I hope it's not too late to find that puzzle."

Catching on quickly, his boss ran out of the station, right behind the younger officer.

When Mable and Archie returned from the theater, the Open Arms owner greeted them at the door, and they noticed new staff. Nurses Lewis and Hamstein were nowhere to be found. But, in Mable's room sat a massive bouquet and a card that simply said "Thank you." Archie and Mable hugged each other and felt safer than they had in days.

***

THE NEXT DAY in the garden sat Archie, Mable, Chief Inspector Saunders, and Sergeant Davis, sipping lemonade. Now there was no reason to whisper.

"So, we were right. Nurse Hamstein was faking the medical records and taking painkillers for herself?" asked Archie.

"Yes, she was," answered the sergeant gently.

"But, she wasn't the one who poisoned Sylvia?" asked Mable.

"Nope," said the sergeant, this time with an ornery grin.

"Young man, are you going to explain things or not?" Mable scolded him while smiling and sipping her drink.

"At first, we thought she might have, but then when we saw that Sylvia had more staff secrets, we realized who had the most to lose," said Chief Inspector Saunders. There was a slight pause to allow Archie and Mable to work it out independently.

"You mean Nurse Lewis?" Mable asked.

"I knew it," demanded Archie. "When she never let me have a second hashbrown, I knew she was a mean one."

The officers smiled, and the boss continued. "We checked out her house and found what she used to poison Sylvia, growing right there in her home."

"What?" Archie asked.

"Well, can you tell us the name of the poison, Inspector?" asked Mable.

"Ricin," he said. Two blank faces stared back at him, so he continued. "It's a poison extracted from the bean of the castor oil plant."

Archie and Mable gasped. Mable sat back in her chair with her jaw hanging down, and eyes opened wide.

"But, how?" Archie asked.

"Usually, it's injected, but as a nurse, she knew someone would discover an injection site. So, she laced the puzzle pieces with it."

"You mean that the whole time Sylvia was putting that beautiful puzzle together, she was slowly poisoning her?" asked Archie.

"How wicked," exclaimed Mable.

The officers got up to leave, and the two retirement lodgers followed them to the front lawn. Before getting into their car, Sergeant Davis looked back and added one more comment.

"You've got it made here now. New staff and I hear you are getting quite a reduced rate."

Archie and Mable shushed him. "Keep that to yourselves, or our deaths will be the next you'll be investigating."

MYSTERY WEEKEND AT MOREHEAD MANSION

MYSTERY WEEKEND AT MOREHEAD MANSION

Twelve crystal wine glasses neatly aligned on a tray swiftly moved through the heavily wallpapered rooms carried by Nellie. Her fair complexion, blonde upswept hair, and young age hid many secrets. She gracefully walked in black heels, matching her maid uniform, complete with a white apron and little white bow in her hair, lined on the edges with black satin. As she moved through a threshold lined with drawn curtains on each side made of burgundy felt, she turned sharply to the right and into the dining room.

A large table sat in the center, covered in a gold-colored cloth with burgundy fringe. Fine china lined the place settings outlined with silver utensils reflecting the dancing flames from the fireplace and candelabras. Nellie glanced approvingly over the table as she slid the last glass into place, obsessively in line with the others. She nodded and began to return to the kitchen when she noticed Ollie, the groundkeeper, switching the sign above the grand front door on the front porch. He secured it into place, stepped down from a stool, and opened the screen door as she smiled at him from the other side.

"Howdy, Miss Nellie," he said, tipping his weathered hat. His skin was a rough age of some sixty-plus years, but everyone knew he was gentle inside. Ollie took care of all the grounds and house maintenance.

"Hello, Ollie," she said with a youthful smile. "Morehead Mansion this weekend, right?"

"That's right," he confirmed.

"That's the hardest part for me," she explained. "Remembering the name week to week."

"I'm sure it's a challenge, but I haven't heard you slip up yet," he said.

"And I don't intend to, ever," she said, smiling as she lifted the empty tray back up on the palm of her hand and swiftly made her way through the house.

This weekend, the property was named Morehead Mansion. Three stories high, it was a stately structure built of red brick and stone. Steeply slanted gables formed several pinnacles with more windows than one could count. The road approaching the mansion crossed a lake of reasonable depth by an old, wooden bridge that seemed to give a bit too much under the weight of a vehicle.

That thought didn't escape the mind of seventeen-year-old Noah Ames, who accompanied his older brother, Danny, and three of his friends. Theo, Jenson, and Cody, all eighteen years of age, considered themselves escape room geniuses. Having conquered all escape rooms within a one-hour radius, they now set their sights on a much more significant and prestigious challenge.

Danny pulled up to the massive manor and parked in a spot marked for guests. As they each exited the car and grabbed their overnight bags, their eyes surveyed the structure and property. Noah lagged as the others climbed the front porch stairs and stood in front of the grand door. Danny looked down at his younger brother.

"Come on," he said. "The house won't gobble you up." The others laughed. Noah climbed the stairs as he squinted his eyes in response to their teasing.

"Maybe you should have stayed at home," sneered Theo.

"I don't think that would have worked out too good for you guys if I had," retaliated Noah with confidence.

Theo stepped forward to challenge Noah, but the younger one stood his ground. The older brother took charge.

"Theo," said Danny. "You know very well that we'll need him here. He saved our butts two escape rooms ago, and you know it."

Theo backed away slightly to appease his friend, and Danny rang the bell. "We would have gotten there," Theo whispered to Noah.

"In your dreams," Noah whispered back. "You never could figure out a puzzle based on calculus."

They looked at each other in surprise at the resounding gong of the bell. The door swung open slowly, and a surly-looking older man in a black suit greeted them with the sourest face they had ever seen. His voice had a monotone stuck in one low octave.

"Good evening, gentlemen," said the old man. "Please come in. You are expected. I am Ambrose, the butler."

They each stepped onto the parquet wood floor, gawking at the lavish interior. Once given their room assignments and a map of the mansion's inside, they were invited to inspect their rooms. As they walked up a carpeted set of stairs, the butler provided them with additional information.

"Dinner will be served in the dining room at seven thirty, and if you are interested, refreshments will be served in the library immediately before and after." Then, the somber butler strolled out of the foyer with panther-like silence, leaving the guys alone heading to the second floor.

***

UPSTAIRS, THEY EACH WALKED the hall to find their rooms. Before entering them, they stood in the hallway talking.

"I don't know about you guys, but that butler creeps me out," said Jenson. Blond curls laid over his eyes as he spoke and stood in his typical hand-in-jean-pocket stance. Jenson was the tallest of the five with a slim build.

"Butlers are supposed to be creepy," laughed Cody. At that moment, his eyes widened in appreciation of a welcome sight. Cody always had an eye for pretty girls. He never talked to them, but he sure could spot them.

A petite, dark-haired girl of about twenty walked down the hall from an undisclosed location. She had on a uniform of pink cotton, and her badge said she was a maid. She smiled brightly at them and was carrying folded white towels.

"Hello," she said. "I'm Sally, your maid for the weekend. If you need anything in your rooms, I'll take care of it for you."

Being the flirt of the group, Theo looked at her badge and coyly spoke to her with a grin.

"Thank you, Sally," he said, donning a smile and a quick wink. "We will let you know."

She smiled at each of them and turned and walked down the hall lined with a plush carpet with an ostentatiously bold print. She turned the corner at the end of the hall, and they resumed their room search.

"This place is so old-fashioned. I mean," Jenson continued, "just look at this carpet. What a crazy print."

"I think it's cool," said Noah.

His older brother smiled at him. "Me too. Come on, guys," he continued. "Let's put our things in our rooms and get down in the library to see what's going on."

Illustrated by: Katie Mylius

They each looked at their rooms, where they dropped off their overnight bags. One by one, they walked past a king-sized bed, lavish furnishings, and a bathroom of equal comparison. None of them remembered staying in any place as fancy as Morehead Mansion. They regrouped in the hall and made their way downstairs.

***

DOWN IN THE LIBRARY, the five guests assembled. Jenson sat tinkering a baby grand piano. Theo and Cody strolled past filled bookshelves on either side of the room. Danny looked out of the window, considering the storm's strength outside. Noah found a seat on a rather plush overstuffed couch, taking in the details of the room as he did most of the time. Observational skills and attention to detail seemed woven into his personality.

"Good thing we're in here," Danny said to anyone who was listening. "Quite a storm is brewing out there."

Noah eyed drinks on the sideboard and jumped up with a smile when he rightly spotted lemonade. After finding ice in a bucket, he poured himself a large glass and turned to continue surveying the whole room.

He noticed the two large windows that overlooked the gardens on one wall, two walls lined with bookshelves, and the fourth wall behind him with the sideboard and door through which they entered from the hall. The far wall, lined with dark paneling around the windows, appealed to his liking. However, he noticed a slight offset between two wall panels. Realizing the others did not see, he decided to stroll over in the direction, pretending to appreciate a painting upon that same wall. After realizing that it was most likely a hidden door, he decided to hold on to the knowledge for the time being. It might end up being important later.

Cody joined Danny at one of the large windows. "Look at that wind," he observed. The high wind slammed buckets of rain against the side of the house. "That bridge we crossed on our way here didn't look all that sturdy to me. If this keeps up, it's liable to be washed out." Danny threw a fearful glance in response as the stern butler appeared at the threshold, taking them by surprise.

"That bridge is often washed away," he said. "They keep rebuilding it, and the weather keeps destroying it," Ambrose spoke in the same monotone and dry manner as usual.

"Well then," answered Cody, "I would say they need to rebuild it with concrete and bricks then."

"Yes, sir," Ambrose answered coldly. "If you would follow me into the dining room, dinner will now be served."

One by one, they each strolled through the hall and into the dining room. Nellie placed the final place card on the table set with fine china, shining silver, and lit candelabras. They each took their assigned seats, and Nellie began placing soup bowls in front of each guest. Noah took no time in digging in as the older boys smiled. Soon, he realized the others stared at him and raised his head.

"What?" he asked in defense.

"Nothing," said his older brother, Danny.

The rest of the table guests laid the cloth napkins on their laps, and Noah, taking a short break, eventually did the same.

"I wonder when the game will start," remarked Jenson, blowing his soup carefully not to burn his mouth.

"I think it's already started," said Cody with a grin.

"Yeah," agreed Danny. "I'm sure it started as soon as we got here."

At that moment, the door opened and Nellie, accompanied by Ambrose, carried in trays with the main course. The aroma filled the air as plates of prime rib and potatoes sat before them. Each of them eagerly devoured their meals in delight, among very little chatting. The guys were just as good at putting away food as they were solving escape room puzzles.

They sipped drinks and set the cloth napkins back upon the table as they each finished. The older boys breathed heavily, indicating they were full. On the other hand, Noah continued with a plate of fruit that sat in the middle of the table. The others laughed under their breath at him.

"What?" Noah asked for the second time.

"Nothing," said Jenson. "You have a very healthy appetite."

"And why is that a problem?" he asked. "I'm a growing boy."

Ambrose returned to the room and stood quietly in the corner, making the boys very uncomfortable. At first, they tried ignoring him, but this became almost impossible. Being the least inhibited, Noah looked at him and asked him a direct question.

"Are you monitoring our conversations?" he asked with a smile.

"No, sir," said Ambrose after a slight pause. "I am to be available, should anyone need any assistance."

"I see," added Cody. "It's very formal here. At least we are getting our money's worth."

After finishing his fruit bowl, Noah seemed satisfied, sitting up straight. He looked back toward Ambrose without hesitation.

"Ambrose," he said, "that was a great meal." The others nodded in agreement.

"I'm glad you enjoyed it. I shall pass that on to the cook," said Ambrose with a bow. "If you are finished, you may wish to retire to the library again."

There was no question in his tone. Instead, he spoke with certainty. No one questioned, so they all rose from their seats and walked somberly back into the library. Obviously, they were being led by some sort of script, but they enjoyed playing along. They each, however, were startled in response to something found proudly sitting to one side, in front of a bookshelf in the library.

***

"WHAT IS THIS?" asked Theo, rubbing his chin.

"How interesting," said Jenson. "I'm not sure."

One by one, they each took a spot surrounding the large, colorful, four-sided object. Standing between the box and bookshelves, Danny spoke with confidence and certainty.

"It's a Chinese puzzle box," he advised.

Illustrated by: Thamia Martinez Caldwell

Jenson laughed. "How do you know that?"

"Well," Danny answered, "I have seen them before, however not this large. But, the best clue would be the note pinned to the back of it stating it's a Chinese puzzle box." Danny pulled the note off the backside of the box while the other four looked from one to the other, grinning.

Danny read the note aloud.

"Please enjoy this giant Chinese puzzle box. You never know what could be a clue. The clever thinker shall be the sly fox. And will separate one from the few." He looked up and then back to the paper. "It's signed, Anne."

For a few seconds, they stood in silence, thinking over the quip. Danny scratched his head sat down in a straightback chair, rereading the clue in the form of a poem. He began to repeat it under his breath.

"Well, you can definitely say that the game has begun," said Cody with a smile. He then looked up to the ceiling, unsure whom he addressed, and raised his voice slightly. "And whoever you are, Anne, thank you for the clue."

"I have an idea," said Danny. "How about we each take a

line to dissect it?"

"Don't you think we need to figure out what the riddle as a whole means?" Jenson argued an excellent point.

"OK," said Theo. "I have an idea. Each of us will take a line, and Noah will study it from a whole perspective. That way, we're coming at it from every angle."

After assigning each of the older boys a line, it became apparent that the first line didn't have much to study. So, Theo and Cody agreed to review line two together. That left line three for Danny, line four for Jenson, and Noah was to look at it in total. Theo and Cody talked about things they would never know about the mansion. Their conversation seemed endless, and they took it off to the sitting room.

Danny began to search the house for pictures, paintings, or statues of a fox. Jenson repeated the last line over and over, talking to himself about the words. Realizing he was in the library by himself, the young guest walked over to the Chinese Box, circled it, carefully studying each side. He spoke softly under his breath.

"What secrets do you have hidden inside, my dear?"

***

Noah stomped up the stairs toward the bedrooms, reeling in anger, full knowing they gave him the whole poem as a sort of consolation prize. Theo never did seem to appreciate how much Noah contributed to the group. *How stupid do they think I am? We'll see who the stupid ones are.*

Noah walked the hall, looking for something or someone. None of the bedroom doors were open. He sighed, realizing he probably had missed Sally, already cleaning the rooms earlier. Just at that moment, he heard a noise coming from behind him. He took a deep breath and turned. Smiling, he was face to face with the lovely Sally. He couldn't put together from where she had come.

"Hello," she said. "Can I get you something?"

"Yeah," he answered. "First, can you tell me where you just came from?"

She smiled. "Why does that matter?"

"OK," he conceded. "Forget that. Just tell me who's Anne."

Sally's eyes became wide. "No one lives here by that name."

Noah found her answer to be very strange. He thought for a moment and then followed up. "I didn't ask you who lived here. I didn't think any of you lived here." He paused and then continued. "Does anyone actually live here?"

"No," she answered timidly. She started to walk away, but he stopped her, lightly grabbing her arm.

"OK," he said. "Let me start over. "Do you know of anyone connected with Morehead Mansion named Anne?"

She looked up and down the hall with fierce eyes glancing. "Not here. Can we talk in your room?"

Nodding, he opened his door with his room key and stepped back, allowing the maid to walk in first. After closing the door, he asked her if she wanted to sit down in one of the easy chairs placed by the fireplace. After sitting, she took a deep breath.

"What are you afraid of?" Noah asked the pretty young maid.

"I can't be seen giving any help," she explained. "The puzzles are meant to be tough. I don't want to get fired."

"Are there any listening devices in the bedrooms?" Noah asked this while looking around the room.

"No, we're safe in here," she answered. She took a deep breath and began. "Anne Morehead was the lady who built this mansion. She lived to be in her eighties. She loved this place, but she left without telling the servants where she was going one day and never returned." Both paused before she finished her story. "No one ever found out what happened to her."

He studied her face while the information circled in his head. After about twenty seconds, she continued the conversation.

"Why are you asking me about Anne?"

"The first clue to open the Chinese Box was signed 'Anne.' All the others are convinced the clue is in the riddle, but I thought maybe it was more important who it was from." He realized they were looking into each other's eyes, and he couldn't help but smile.

Just at that moment, they both jumped at a knock that came upon his bedroom door. She jumped up in fear. He must have read her mind.

"Don't worry," he said. "I won't tell anyone that you helped me."

Feeling terrified, she ran into the bathroom and grabbed a

towel. Then, she gestured for him to open the door. In the hallway stood the other four in his party. When they saw her, they donned ornery grins. Sally turned to Noah, holding up the towel.

"I am so sorry the towel was stained," she contended. "I'll get you a clean one." She then moved toward the door and walked out into the hall as the other guys moved back to allow her to pass.

Jenson was the first to tease. "A towel, huh?" He snickered. "Good way to lure her to your room, you dog."

"Stop it," he argued. "It was just a stained towel." Noah appeared genuinely serious about defending the maid's reputation.

"OK, OK," said Danny. "Well, we aren't getting anywhere with the riddle tonight. We thought maybe we would play some cards and go to bed."

"Where?" asked Noah.

"In my room," said Danny.

"OK, I'll be right in," said Noah.

***

THE FIVE GUYS SAT around a round table in Danny's room, each taking turns slamming cards down. Jenson was right at home, animated and loud. One of them had to shush him for fear of breaking some unknown noise rule in the mansion every few minutes. Jenson continued to be loud, and no one came to silence them.

Noah never really cared for playing cards, but he went along with them anyway. Frequently, he eyed the clock ticking behind Jenson on a dresser, hoping they would soon become tired and decide to go to bed. This would allow him to search the house for information on Anne Morehead, namely in the library. Jenson continued to beg for one more hand, but the others began to yawn. Noah immediately fake-yawned in step with the others as if right on cue.

After making sure the others were in their rooms, Noah crept out of his room as silently as he could, making sure not to make a noise with the door. He chose to exchange jeans for sweatpants as he felt this might allow him more room to move freely. He crept through the darkness feeling the wall, misjudging the distance to the steps as he took two additional baby steps before reaching the edge, the whole time convinced he would misstep and plummet to the bottom of the stairs.

Fearful of falling, he took the staircase very slowly, wishing he would have thought to count them during the day. Once at the bottom, he prowled forward in the direction of the library. Once past the doorway, he carefully shut the door and reached into his pocket for his cell phone to use the flashlight. The last thing he wanted to do was to alert anyone. Explaining his presence to Ambrose might be difficult. He began his search through the bookcases, looking for anything that might help him learn more about the mansion's previous owner.

He happened upon two books on the history and unexplained mysteries related to the town. He nearly skipped the last shelf; however, he couldn't believe his eyes and luck when he found an old, leatherbound, tattered book entitled *Morehead Mansion*. It was the very last book on the very last shelf.

"Jackpot!" he exclaimed under his breath and then looked around him to ensure no one was watching. All seemed well in the silent darkness. Moving books over to hide the spaces left, he decided to take them to his room.

While he drifted near the staircase, his eyes caught sight of a portrait hanging off to the right. He figured he must have seen it earlier, but it now stood out for some reason. He crept closer and shined his dim flashlight onto it, sliding the beam slowly to the bottom. Under the ornate frame, written on a nameplate, was "Anne Morehead, 1925." Swallowing hard, he rose the beam of light back up to the face of the woman, dressed in what looked to be a velvet floor-length dress with an unusually high neckline. No one he knew would dress that way now, but it reminded him of pictures in his history book at school.

However, he reached out his left arm to grab the wood banister and shuddered at touching some unknown object. He nearly jumped when he realized he was handling the suit jacket of a worker. Strangely, this worker did not move or flinch. Noah gasped when his flashlight hit the stone-like face of Ambrose, the butler. Noah couldn't help but wonder what kept him from jumping in surprise. It was like he was a robot and not a real person.

"Oh, Ambrose," stammered Noah. "You scared the life out of me."

"Sorry, sir," said Ambrose, monotone and bland as one could imagine speaking. One couldn't help but also wonder how he spoke without moving facial muscles, except for the lips.

"What are you doing here?" asked Noah, realizing the butler probably was wondering the same about him.

"I heard a noise and came to check that everything was alright," he explained.

"Oh, of course," answered Noah. "I came to get a couple of books to read. Insomnia, you know."

"Yes, sir," repeated Ambrose. As Noah began to ascend the stairs, the butler continued. "Good night, sir," and as fast as Noah could turn his head to look behind and downward, Ambrose was no longer standing in the foyer.

Noah turned around and quickly glided up the stairs and lost no time entering his bedroom. He sighed in relief and set the books down on his bed. Allowing his eyes to pass over them each one by one, it suddenly occurred to him that it was well after midnight, and Ambrose had been wearing his tuxedo. Noah shook his head, lay back on the bed, and raised a book above him. He thought to himself. *He probably sleeps in it.* Coincidentally, he did the same, falling asleep on top of his covers.

***

THEY ROSE TO FIND the rain had not yet let up the following day. Danny looked out his second-story window as he buttoned up his shirt. He saw water lying in puddles throughout the gardens and realized the flooding might become a severe issue. He went to grab his cell phone but then dropped it back onto his bed after remembering the rules.

Everyone looked rested except for Noah, who rubbed his red, irritated eyes, meeting the others in the hallway. Having endured teasing about Sally being in his room the previous day, he and the others walked down the stairs and in the direction of the dining room. Noah trailed last but turned to look at the portrait he discovered the previous night in daylight. Baffled at seeing a landscape instead, furtive glances around the room communicated his anxiety.

Ambrose mysteriously showed up at the far end of the foyer and cleared his throat. Noah turned to speak to him.

"Where's the portrait of Anne Morehead?" he asked, pointing up at the landscape.

"Sir?" asked Ambrose.

"The portrait that was up here last night; the one of Anne Morehead dated 1925."

"Oh," appeased Ambrose. "You must be referring to the one that hangs in the library."

"No," said Noah with a slightly condescending tone. "I'm referring to the one that was hanging here last night."

Ambrose stepped in the direction of the library and lifted his hand to guide Noah's gaze. No amount of frustration ruffled the feathers of this butler. The young guest reluctantly walked over and peered into the room. He looked from the painting to Ambrose and back again.

Oh," he said with a grin while crossing his arms over his chest. "You guys are good."

"Good, sir?" asked the butler.

"Moving that picture was a sneaky move."

Ambrose didn't respond except for a slight raise of his eyebrows. Noah was in disbelief, now bordering on anger.

"You're telling me that you never moved that painting, that it's been hanging there on that wall all the time?"

Again, Ambrose did not respond except for a raise of the eyebrows.

Noah smiled widely this time. "Oh, you guys really are very, very good at this."

"Um, yes sir, if you say so," answered the butler. "Now, if you will follow me, you can join your party for breakfast."

Noah did so and found his friends sitting around the big dining room table once again, this time waiting for omelets and toast. Glasses of orange juice sat at each setting, and Noah took his place in the empty chair. This time, he remembered to lay the cloth napkin on his lap like the others.

"Where were you?" asked Cody.

At that moment, Ambrose entered from the kitchen with Nellie close behind him, pausing their conversation. Plates filled with omelets, sausage, and toast were laid before each of them. Talking was replaced by munching and sipping. Ambrose stood as still as a statue in the corner of the room, as he did the previous evening.

"Ambrose," said Danny, "may I have more juice?" He gestured toward his empty juice glass.

"Of course, sir," the butler dryly answered as he sauntered from the room. Despite being an inside room with no windows, cracks of lightning, wind, and pelting rain could be heard. Theo's eyes widened as he listened.

"Boy, do I have a lot to fill you guys in on," whispered Noah after checking that they were alone.

"We're meeting in Jenson's room after breakfast," directed Cody.

Noah nodded, and Ambrose reentered the room with a pitcher full of a brightly orange-colored beverage. He diligently refilled each of their glasses and returned to his post in the corner. Satisfying their healthy appetites, they finished their plates in silence and raced up the stairs to Jenson's room to discuss matters.

***

"YOU'RE TELLING US," asked Theo, "that the picture you saw in the foyer in the middle of the night is now in the library?"

"That's right," Noah answered. "And Ambrose acted like it's always been in there. But I *know* it was in the foyer last night. I'm sure."

"I believe you," said Danny.

"Me too," said Cody and Theo, nearly in unison.

"Well, I guess," admitted Jenson, "moving the picture could be a part of the mystery." As he spoke, he gently tossed the curtain tassel through his fingers, paying close attention to the severity of the storm.

"Speaking of the mystery," said Danny authoritatively, "has anyone made any headway with that first clue?"

Each answered with heads moving back and forth, indicating no, so Noah knew he would have to spill a few of the beans in his pocket.

"Well, I decided to focus on the name Anne at the bottom of the clue." Noah was surprised at the response from his cohorts.

"The name doesn't matter," insisted Jenson. "It's decoding the clues that are important here. I mean, it's obvious that we need to get the giant Chinese puzzle box open, and to do that, we need to figure out the meaning of each clue."

"Hold on. Hold on," said Danny. "Noah might be onto something here. The writer included the name in the clue so it could matter. Who's to say the name of the person providing the clue isn't important?"

"Thank you," Noah directed at his older brother.

"You're welcome," Danny responded. "Now, how do we talk to this Anne?"

"Well, we don't," Noah said meekly. "She's the lady who built the house. And, she's dead."

"What?" yelled Jenson, tossing the tassel aside permanently. "You see. It's a dead end, literally."

"Not necessarily," Noah retorted with matching volume. "I found books on her in the library in this very house. I'm reading them to see if they can help us with the riddle."

Jenson brushed back dark thick hair from his forehead in frustration, shaking his head.

"Now, Jenson," said Theo. "It could lead somewhere. I say we let Noah read the books to see if he finds out anything useful. Meanwhile, the four of us can return down to the library to take another look at this box. A close look."

"I agree," said Cody.

Jenson reluctantly agreed also. "Whatever. I don't have any better ideas."

Noah returned to his room and sprawled out on his bed, reading page after page. Thirst crept in, so he opened cupboard door after cupboard door until he found the mini fridge and some bottled water. At the same time, the four walked downstairs into the library, to yet another surprise left for them—the second clue.

***

Cody, Theo, and Danny walked into the library beside the oversized Chinese puzzle box. Jenson stayed back in the foyer, investigating the landscape painting Noah talked about earlier. Jenson leaned in to inspect it in detail, and then from the side, squinting his eyes as he tried to spot its connection to the wall. Rejoining the others in the library, he immediately turned to the left, away from the puzzle box, to examine the portrait of Anne Morehead.

Having completed his assessment, he turned to see the other three gaping at another white paper. Danny held it with the other two standing on either side. Realizing it was the second clue, Jenson wasted no time getting over with them.

"Another clue?" he asked without expecting an answer. He joined them, and Danny read aloud.

" Work as a team to avoid a fight. It's a love for the old hidden in plain sight. Take a seat and find the dove. Not on the left or right, but from above."

"This is terrible," yelled Jenson, slapping his hands against his legs in despair. "We haven't even figured out the first clue, and now we have the second one. We're bombing."

"Don't be such a drama queen," teased Theo. "Freaking out isn't going to help anything."

"Theo's right," Cody agreed. "Maybe we can move on to the second clue and come back to the first later."

"Have you ever seen any escape room puzzles solved out of sequence?" asked Jenson arrogantly.

"No," said Danny. "But, this isn't your ordinary escape room, is it?"

"I don't see that we have any other choice," argued Cody.

Jenson lowered his head in defeat, wiped his sweaty forehead, and walked toward one of the windows. Picking up a magazine, he began to fan himself. Ambrose slipped into the room and straightened the line of beveled glasses sitting on the sideboard. Something out of the corner of his eye concerned him, and he jerked around.

"Young man," Ambrose demanded loudly. Startled, they all jerked their bodies, as they had never heard the butler speak with any amount of emotion since arriving. "What are you doing?"

Jenson, whose hand was unfastening the window lock, froze but was too late. Everyone in the room stood still, listening intently to what sounded like metal locks echoing shut throughout the large mansion. Once they stopped, the foursome did not break their statue impressions. Ambrose, on the other hand, hung his head in despair.

"What was that?" Jenson asked Ambrose.

"That was the sound of every door and window lock in the house clicking shut, along with bars covering the outside of every window and door as well."

Great," said Cody. "Now, we're locked in."

"What does it matter?" asked Danny, sitting down and rolling his eyes. "It's not like we're going anywhere anytime soon."

"What do you mean?" asked Jenson. "We can leave any time we want. That's what it said on the website."

Jenson looked at Ambrose, who refused to explain. So, the loud youngster did so himself.

"What Ambrose isn't telling us is that the bridge is already washed out, isn't it?"

***

NOAH SNAPPED UPRIGHT on his bed upstairs after hearing the massive snapping of the locks. A dark cast emanating from his window drew him in as he slowly walked over. His brow furrowed in confusion as he leaned in to investigate. He could barely see anything through what looked like thick metal bars covering the window. Walking downstairs, the sound of his steps clambered loudly throughout a silent mansion.

Four friends and the butler stood staring at one another when

Noah walked past a landscape photo in the foyer and then over the threshold into the library. He gained no answers, looking from one to another. Bars across the library windows didn't escape his notice, and at that moment, he knew they were totally locked inside.

Danny raised his hand, holding the second clue, Noah's cue to come to look. Taking the paper from Danny, he noticed Ambrose moving behind him. The butler stopped and faced Danny and his little brother.

"I'm needed in the kitchen," the stoic butler stated, bowed, and stepped back and out the door.

"No point worrying about the doors and locks," said Theo. "It's just part of the weekend mystery, so let's just work together and focus on the clue."

"Pointless," argued an angry Jenson. He shot daggers with his eyes toward the four. "We didn't make any progress on the first clue. Zilch!"

Cody stepped forward. "I don't know about the rest of you, but I came here to conquer this mystery weekend. The only way we have a chance of doing that is to get moving on any and every clue we can. The order doesn't matter to me. Let's just get on with it."

Theo, Danny, and Noah grinned, nodded, and bent forward with Cody to reread and study clue number two. Jenson rose and reluctantly joined his friends.

"Good," said Cody. "We managed to avoid a fight, as the clue states. Now, let's move on to finding something that's old."

"There are tons of old things in this place, including Ambrose," joked Danny, adding some much needed fun. "Guess we need to figure out which items are the oldest. I'm not sure how we're going to do that."

Jenson added a thought. "It says we need to take a seat. Maybe it's a piece of furniture you sit on."

"Well," added Noah, "it says to sit down, but then it says to find the dove from above."

"And?" asked Danny.

"Sitting doesn't mean you sit on it," Noah explained. "You could sit on the floor and look up at it and see a dove."

"Great," sighed Theo as he sat down on a chair. "That means it could be virtually anything."

After a short silent pause, Danny walked into the center of the room and suggested, "OK. I have an idea. They gave us all maps when we arrived. How about dividing up the rooms and making up a list of the oldest things in each room? And if anyone sees a dove, make a note of that too."

"Do you know how long that will take?" Jenson continued to display his lousy attitude.

"It will take a lot less time divided by five of us instead of four," Danny calmly explained. He then walked over to an end table and picked up his drink. "Two of us can search all the rooms on this level."

"I'll work on that with you," offered Theo.

"Who wants to search the second floor with me?" asked Cody.

"I can," Jenson reluctantly offered.

"There might be an attic and a basement," Noah added. "I'll see if I can find out and search them."

"Let's get at it and meet back here," suggested Danny. "Text when you each finish."

With that, they each went their separate ways and began the

search. Noah made his way straight upstairs to find his inside contact, Sally.

***

ONCE MAKING SURE Cody and Jenson were searching inside second-floor rooms, he walked to the area in the hall from where he once saw Sally enter. After turning the corner, he softly knocked on the wall, looking around him. The wall, which was a door, opened quickly to his surprise, and Sally stood before him in her usual maid's outfit.

"Hi, Noah," greeted Sally with a smile. Noah couldn't help but smile back at the pretty face but soon found his footing.

"Hi," he repeated back. "Listen, I need a little more help," he said, looking around to make sure no one heard. "We need to search every room in the house to have any chance of solving the clues."

"Why do you need to search every room in the house?"

"The second clue said we need to find something that's old. I'm in charge of finding out if there's an attic or a basement and searching them."

"I see," answered Sally. She stepped back and gestured for him to come into the room.

He realized he was standing inside a huge maids' workroom as he stepped in. In the far corner stood an oversized washer and dryer, buzzing. Near them and to the right were shelves packed full of detergent and other types of cleaners. Beyond them were large counters and tables, perfect for folding the wash, and then finally, there were closets presumably filled with clean towels and linens.

The diligent maid took a load of towels from the dryer, laid them on the countertop, and began to fold. After Noah surveyed the room, he turned to her and noticed she was still smiling at him.

"What?" he asked.

"You look younger than your friends," she said.

"I am. They're eighteen, and I'm seventeen. Danny's my older brother. You don't look all that old."

"I'll be nineteen in one month."

"How long have you been working here?" asked Noah.

"I'm here just for the summer. I'm in college, studying art." She grabbed sheets and pillowcases from a cupboard. "Did you have any questions for me related to the mystery weekend?"

"Yes, I do. So, will you tell me if there's an attic or basement?" he asked as his hands slid into his jean pockets.

Smiling didn't cease as she answered. "Yes, I'll help you, but you can't tell anyone. Like I said before, I don't want to get into any trouble."

"Deal," he agreed. "So?"

"There are both an attic and a basement. As it happens, the attic door is right there," she said, pointing over toward what looked like cupboard doors. It's pretty tiny."

He walked in the direction of her pointing but found himself looking from one door to the next and then looking back to her.

She laughed. "The middle door, but if you get caught, you sneaked in here and found it all on your own, OK?"

"Of course," he said with a smile before opening the door and bolting up the stairs.

At the top of the stairs, he found a small room lined with boxes, chairs, and tables. He walked from item to item, taking a good look, and then reluctantly sat on the dirty and dusty floor and looked up underneath the tables. Dejected, he returned to the maids' workroom and found he was now alone. He grabbed what looked like a cleaning rag and wiped dirt from his clothes, wishing he would have asked Sally for the location of the basement door. He did have an idea.

He was stunned through the hallway and downstairs to the main floor, not running into anyone, not Ambrose or any of his four friends. As he walked through the foyer, he stopped short in shock as he looked up at the portrait of Anne Morehead. He knew it had to be up again for a reason.

"I'll deal with you later," he said to the painting. "Right now, I'm on a mission."

Quietly, he opened the library door, stepped in, and shut it behind him, confirming it was empty. It was dark with all the windows covered in bars, so he turned on a lamp and glided to the wall he was eyeing before. With his flat palm, he caressed the wallpaper and trim, searching for the area that looked offset. His fingernails lingered on a piece of trim. As he rolled his hands up and down the frame, he stopped occasionally and applied pressure. Eventually, a trim piece slid away from the wall and was hinged. Once loosened, the fake wall, also hinged, spun open with little force.

He gingerly walked in through into a dark space. Not wanting to get stuck, he took a pen out of his pocket and wedged it into the opening. After summoning the flashlight on his cell phone, he realized a set of steps were in front of him. He didn't know if this was *the* basement, but he knew it was *a* basement. The decorations and furniture stored below were of a different style, more modern and straightforward. Soon, he stopped in front of a desk with shelves sitting on top.

Not sure why he felt this was the one, he sat down in the chair and pointed his flashlight upward. Unsure of what it was, he stood up to get a better view of a small object painted on the wood on the underside of the shelves. He couldn't believe his eyes and whispered out loud.

"A dove," he said under his breath. "It's a dove." He thought long and hard about the clue. "Now that I've found you, my little friend, what now?" He reached up and touched it, and at that moment, a secret compartment opened and revealed a folded piece of paper. He sat back down, propped his phone up to show light on the desktop, unfolded the letter, and read it aloud.

"So you found your way here, but now it's time to zoom. Follow the hallway to the right and take this paper back to your room."

Without hesitation, he did as the paper instructed. The dark and dingy hallway began to incline, and, as he guessed, it led to another secret opening exiting in the hall on the second floor. After securing the fake wall in place, he entered his room, sat on a chair, and reread the clue. This time, his eyes noticed some writing on the lower end of the paper.

"Noellen."

"What?" He scratched his head, fearing all his great investigative work was nothing short of a waste of time.

***

AFTER SENDING A GROUP TEXT, he and his crew sat around his room. He shared his adventures and then suddenly realized he had left a pen in the wall opening in the library. Jenson ran down to look, but they all couldn't believe their eyes after he returned. He was unfolding clue #3.

Everyone sighed, but Noah kept his composure. "Just read it."

Instead, Jenson's anger showed its ugliness again. "It's so

hot in here. Maybe I can just crack this little window in the bathroom. It's not like any of us can fit through it." He bolted into the bathroom and tried to unfasten the tiny window. At the same time, he heard his friends shriek from the bedroom. Afraid of what he would find, he slowly walked back. Their eyes bulged as they gazed up toward the ceiling.

Jenson's gaze followed, and he gasped, staring at a knife stuck into the wall near the ceiling. He raised his arms with his palms up and shrugged his shoulders at his friends.

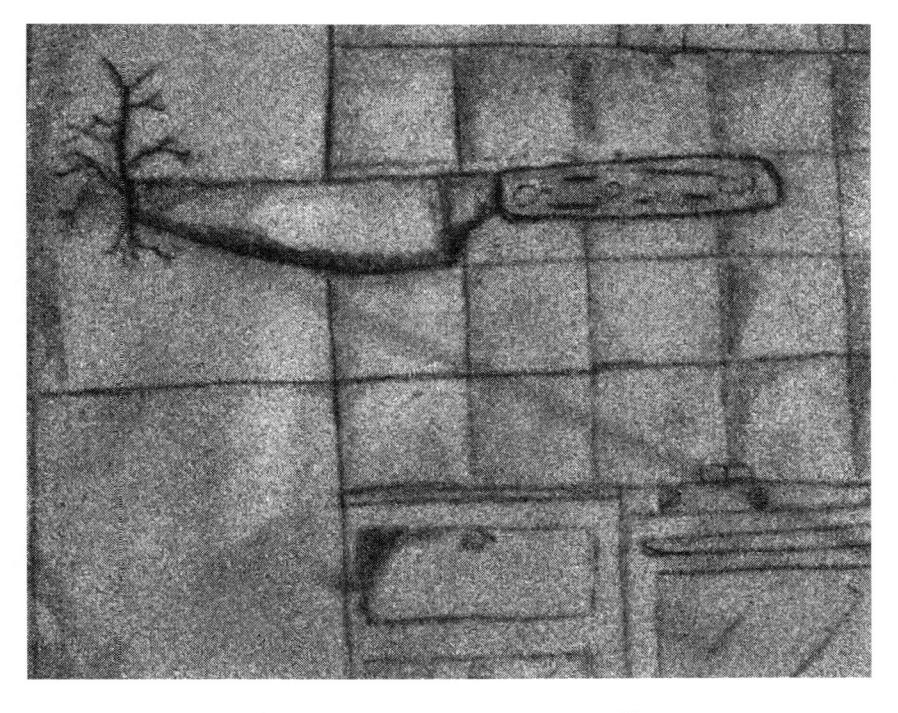

Illustrated by: Rowan Wills

Danny stepped forward. "When will you get it through your thick head that we can't open any windows or doors?" He calmed himself with a deep breath. "OK?"

"Yeah," he said meekly. "OK." He sat down and opened the clue to read. "I wish I would have read this before I tried the window."

"Why?" asked Theo. "What does it say?"

Jenson read aloud. "Best be careful and listen to us. Doors and windows are ominous." He handed it to Theo and lowered his head into his hands.

"Wait a minute," Theo said. "The word ominous is underlined. Maybe that means something."

"Yeah, maybe it means we shouldn't try to open any windows or doors," said Cody sarcastically.

"Funny," interjected Jenson. "You can all stop mocking me now."

"No," explained Theo. "Maybe it means the word is essential to the clues."

The dinner bell rang, and they each realized they were starving, stating "I'm hungry" and "Yeah, I could eat." Maybe, they agreed, letting the information from the clues settle in their heads and some nourishment might help. They ate in silence, each of them knowing it was the second of their three-day mystery weekend. They were no closer to solving any of the clues. Noah ate; however, a lot was going on behind his eyes.

They sat in the library sipping on after-dinner drinks of lemonade, mainly staring toward the floor, looking, in the very least, dejected. Noah was the only one who seemed deep in thought. After some time, and without looking at anyone, he spoke.

"Maybe we should take a look at all three of the clues together on a table," he said.

Almost a full minute later, they each took a seat at a table, and each clue was laid out onto the shiny wood surface one by one. As they sat and looked at them quietly, the silence seemed to envelop them. It was like the clues were the only things in the room. So much that they jumped, startled as Nellie, the downstairs maid, entered the room.

"I'm sorry if I'm disturbing you," she said. "I just wanted to see if there was anything else you required before we clean up in the kitchen for the night."

They each shook their heads no, but Danny rose to speak to her. "No," he said, smiling. "Unless you have the solution to all three of these clues."

"It looks like we won't solve this mystery weekend," sighed Theo.

Cody pursed his lips and added, "Well, at least we had a nice weekend in a really cool mansion."

"I don't have the solution," Nellie said with a smile. "But, I think I have some valuable advice."

The five guys looked around at each other, and Noah shrugged his shoulders and chimed in. "At this point, I'm certainly open to any advice."

"All I can say is that you guys have done better than you think, and right now, what you need is a good night's sleep."

She seemed so serious and sure of herself. Much more certain than they were. Danny couldn't be rude, so he felt it necessary to respond in kind.

"It's nice of you to try to help us," he said. "Thank you."

Nellie dropped her tray from her palm above her head, stepped forward, and drove her point home. "Really," she said, this time dropping her smile to be completely serious. "Go to bed and get a good night's sleep. That's what you all need to do."

***

Noah awoke Sunday morning to the sun peeking through the luxurious curtains covering his bedroom window. He couldn't help but stare at the pattern of light painted on his ceiling. He counted the strange figures created by the sunlight. *One. Two. Three, Four.* The number danced through his mind, and it made him think of the mystery weekend clues. He sighed in disappointment, having not solved them. And today was the last day, Sunday.

After rising and cleaning up, he received a group text from Danny stating they should go to breakfast and pack to leave. After a somber yet hearty breakfast, Ambrose told them they would need to go to the library for instructions for going away due to the bridge being taken out by the storm a few days earlier.

As they strolled toward the library, Jenson complained. "Why can't they just provide us with a map of how to get around the bridge instead of making us all sit through the instructions?"

"Do you have a date or somewhere to be, Jenson? Are you in some kind of hurry?" asked Cody.

"No, it's just ridiculous, that's all."

"We all hate that we didn't solve the clues and break open the box," Cody explained. "Don't be so sore."

After they each sat down, Noah restlessly rose again and walked over to the clues still atop the table where they left them last evening before going to bed as Nellie suggested.

"One last look at the clues, I guess," he said. Then, his eyes widened, and he called to his older brother. "Wait a minute. Danny, come look at this."

Danny joined him, followed by the other three. "What is it?" asked Danny.

"Look," said Noah. "Not only are they in a different order, but there is a fourth one too."

"Great," Jenson yelled, waving his arms in the air. "They

mess up the order and add a fourth one. Nothing like pouring salt in the wounds." Jenson started to move them back in their order last night, but Noah stopped him.

"Stop," he said, grabbing his wrist. "Maybe they are trying to help us. Maybe they're supposed to be in this order."

Noah returned them to the previous order, and they all stared at them for several minutes.

"No," admitted Cody in exasperation. "It's no use. They don't make any sense." He walked over to the sideboard and poured himself a glass of ice water, kept in the crystal carafe upon a tray.

Each one of them moved away from the table, sighing, except for Noah, who stared and stared and stared. He then began to walk around repeating the underlined words in each clue. "Anne." "Ominous." "Noellen." And the fourth and newest one, just added this morning. "Yuno."

Jenson finally lost what little patience he had left. "We might as well forget it, guys," he said in despair. "None of the words make sense. It's a bust. And where is Ambrose with our so-called going away instructions?"

Noah continued to pace and repeat the clue words to himself as if no one else was in the room. Then he ran back over to the table and turned the papers upside down to reveal blank pages. He then searched the room for a marker. He did not find one and called out for Ambrose, who immediately provided him with something with which to write, as if he had pulled it out of a hat along with a rabbit.

Danny followed Noah back to the table. "What are you doing, Noah?"

Noah didn't answer, but Danny watched him as he proceeded to write each of the underlined clue words and phrases on a piece of paper. He then slid them around to see if they made sense once arranged differently. Just as Noah seemed ready to give up, he screamed.

"That's it," he yelled. He grabbed at his hair, looked back at the other four, and repeated. "That's it. I've got it.

"I think I know the solution," he explained. "Danny, help me carry these papers to the floor by the Chinese puzzle box."

They each grabbed two of the four papers and sprawled them out onto the floor beside the box. Cody and Theo moved to get a better view, and Jenson reluctantly followed.

Noah looked from the floor to the box. "We were so fixated on the clues that we never really did get a good look at this box."

"I did," said Jenson. "It's just a jumbled mess as far as I'm concerned."

"It does seem like it's covered with random designs and such," added Cody.

"Yes, it does," agreed Noah. "But, I'm sure these symbols have to stand for something."

"Yeah," offered Theo. "But what?"

Noah pointed to symbols arranged in a row around the center of the four sides. "These stand out," he said. "And I think there is a row of symbols just like these on each side, right?"

Theo, Danny, and Cody stood before the other three sides. "Yes," said Theo. "There is a line of symbols on this side too." The other two agreed.

"There are six in my row," said Noah. "How many in the other rows," he asked of the others.

"Um," said Theo while counting. "Six on mine."

"Mine too," Cody chimed in.

"Wait a minute," exclaimed Danny. "Eight. There's eight on mine."

"Eight?" asked Cody. "Why would there be six on three sides and eight on the fourth? What happened to symmetry?"

Jenson leaned over the couch and grinned and shook his head as if he was sure they wouldn't figure anything out.

"So that adds up to twenty-six." Noah looked back to the ground toward the clue words and then exclaimed. "I got it. Twenty-six. There are twenty-six letters in the English alphabet."

"So what?" asked Jenson. "This is a Chinese puzzle box, remember?"

"Yes," agreed Noah. "But I'm guessing that it was designed by someone who is English speaking."

"Yes," said Cody. "After all, no one we've seen in this house looks to be Chinese, and we're not in China."

"Exactly," agreed Danny. "OK. So, if each symbol represents a letter, how do we find A?"

"Well," said Noah, sauntering around the box. "There has to

be a way to know." When he got to the fourth side, he smiled and looked up. "This is where it starts."

"Now, how in the world can you know that?" asked Jenson.

"Because this is the only side with a sun. Each day begins with the sun rising." Jenson raised his eyebrows, but Noah ignored him and continued. "And we read from left to right, so we go in this direction," he said with his right hand pointing in that same direction.

"OK," offered Cody. "Now, if that's true, what do we do next?"

Noah took a deep breath and looked back at the clue words written in marker on the papers, now laying on the floor. After a few minutes, he began to reveal the answer.

"Anne and Ominous together become *Anonymous*."

"Wow," exclaimed Theo. "That's brilliant. So then Noellen and Yuno become *No one you know.*"

"Yes," exclaimed Cody while pumping his fist. "That's it."

Jenson, clearly starting to become impressed, surprisingly jumped over the back of the couch and joined them.

"So," continued Noah, "to make this easier, I'm marking

each symbol with its corresponding letter beginning on the side with a sun."

Danny smiled at his little brother and patted him on the shoulder. "I'm sure glad we brought you along."

After completing this task, he asked Jenson to read each letter, spelling *Anonymous* and *No one you know.* Jenson agreed, and as he read each letter, his four friends pushed on the symbols corresponding with the letter. As the characters depressed and clicked on the Chinese puzzle box, excitement filled the air in the room. As far as they were concerned, the only things in that room were the five of them and that giant Chinese puzzle box. As the final symbol was depressed, they all heard an overwhelmingly loud click, and the box split in half, revealing an opening.

"We did it," screamed Jenson. The others shot him a sour face. "Well, I helped too."

Danny laughed as the rest of them smiled and rolled their eyes. Danny patted Jenson on the back just like he did to Noah. "Of course you did."

Noah stepped forward and pried open the box the rest of the

way to see inside. He had withdrawn his hands, displaying a set of keys attached to a key holder which read, *Congratulations. You solved the Mystery Weekend at Morehead Mansion.*

Startled, they each snapped their heads around in response to Ambrose, Nellie, and Sally clapping from the other side of the room.

"Congratulations, gentlemen," said Ambrose in his usual dry tone. "Now, you might wish to pack and gather your things."

"But wait," Theo chimed in. "What about the washed-out bridge?"

"Theo," said Noah. "I bet anything there never was a washed-out bridge."

Sally looked directly at Noah. "You are clever, aren't you?"

***

AFTER PACKING, they each carried their overnight bags down to the foyer. Nellie, Ambrose, and Sally stood in a line in front of the landscape picture. Noah looked up at it and laughed under his breath.

Danny stepped forward and stretched out his hand to each of the servants. "Thank you for a very intriguing weekend. Your clues were very challenging."

"Yeah," said Jenson. "Very challenging."

Noah looked at Ambrose. "So," he said. "What's this place going to be called for your next mystery weekend? Let me guess. Motley Manor?"

His friends looked around in surprise and confusion. Ambrose, Nellie, and Sally looked impressed. Theo stepped forward, addressing Noah.

"I don't understand," he said.

"It's simple," said Noah. "They change the name of this place, change the furniture, change the history, and so on for each mystery weekend. I figured that out when I saw all the different types of furniture down in the hidden passageway."

Danny smiled. "And I'll bet you also found a sign that said *Motley Manor* on it too."

"Yep," said Noah with pride. "Sure did.

They each said their goodbyes and started to exit the front door as Ollie, the groundsman, drove up in their vehicle. He jumped out and stepped away, letting Danny enter the driver's side. Before Noah managed to get in, Sally ran up to him and slipped a small piece of paper into his hand.

"What's this?" he asked.

"It's my number. Call me," the upstairs maid said with a smile. "When you turn eighteen, that is."

Noah blushed and smiled back at her. "I will."

THE END

Made in the USA
Middletown, DE
30 March 2022